TRAPPED

SHADOWS OF THE VOID BOOK 7

J.J. GREEN

INFINITEBOOK

BOOKS ORDER

The Books of Shadows of the Void - Complete Series

Prequel: Starbound

Book 1: Generation

Book 2: Stranded

Book 3: Dawn

Book 4: Shadowrise

Book 5: Underworld

Book 6: Burned

Book 7: Trapped

Book 8: Mars Born

Book 9: Shadow Battle

Book 10: Shadow War

Books 1 - 3 The Galathea Chronicles

Books 4 - 7 The Earth Chronicles

Books 8 - 10 The Galactic Chronicles

1

Things were getting desperate. They'd eaten the last of the food two days previously, and the water had run out the day before. Jas sat in the cab of the truck and wondered how much longer they would last if they didn't succeed in breaking through the Shadows' siege of Sayen's home.

Carl had parked the truck a kilometer or so away. Its battery was almost dead. Jas hoped they were far enough from the house to avoid detection. Sayen's call to her parents from the untraceable interface had gone through, and after they'd gotten over their joy at hearing her voice, they'd diverted the call to an encrypted line.

Neither of Sayen's parents had left home for weeks. They hadn't even ordered food deliveries in fear that the Shadows would take the opportunity to invade. The aliens were watching them, they'd said, and though they might have been able to leave, they didn't know where to go or who they could trust. Her parents had activated a force field around the home, but they would momentarily drop their defenses at an agreed time to allow the truck in.

Jas was sure that the minute the Shadows saw the truck, they would recognize it as the one that had been used to steal a Shadow scanner from the spaceport. Maybe they even knew exactly who was inside. Their reach had stretched far—deep into the recesses of the Global Government.

The Shadows were certainly in no doubt about who Sayen Lee was. Their attempt to kill her after she'd breached the Global Government's secure files on them had failed. Jas and Carl had defeated the Shadows in their attempt to take control of the starship *Galathea*. Young Makey, the sole escapee from the Shadow invasion of the colony planet, Dawn, had gone missing from his refugee institution. Perhaps only Erielle, the wounded under-worlder who had helped Jas and the others, was as yet unknown to the aliens.

They were the ones who the Shadows knew had discovered their secret invasion of Earth. They were the ones who were a danger. If they could reach the Transgalactic Council before the Shadows had taken Earth, and bring the might of the Unity military forces down upon the fledgling offensive, the aliens might yet be defeated.

But the group would have one chance and one chance only to reach the safety of Sayen's parents' estate and transmit a deep space comm to the Council.

"What's the time?" Makey asked, though it could be clearly seen on the dashboard. The kid was understandably nervous.

"We've got ten minutes," Carl replied. His arms were resting on the truck's steering wheel as he watched the cars passing.

Jas's tongue and mouth were thick with thirst. Her stomach had given up complaining about its emptiness the day before. Even if they had their credchips, they couldn't buy anything without the Shadows immediately identifying and capturing them. Jas wasn't too concerned about their lack of provisions. If they didn't get inside the Lees' house, they probably wouldn't survive anyway. However, she was worried about Erielle. The woman was still recovering from severe laser burns to both legs. Until the day before last, she'd seemed to be recovering, but the lack of water and food had weakened her far more than the others. She was drifting in and out of consciousness as she lay on the cab floor behind the seats.

"So, where are we going to find our Shadow to scan?" Sayen asked. "If we can't prove to the Council what's happening, there's not a lot of point in my parents sending a deep space packet to them."

"They shouldn't be too hard to find," replied Jas. "I'm guessing it'll be whoever's shooting at us. We just have to capture one without killing it."

"That all?"

"That's all."

"You realize I've gotta raise the shield around the cab before we get close?" Carl asked. "As soon as they see us, they're gonna start firing."

"Krat," Jas said. The laser proof steel wall had protected them on more than one occasion, and they would need it now, but it would deprive everyone but Carl of a view outside. She hadn't figured that into her plan. If it had been just her, she would have taken her chances with no shield, but she didn't want to expose the others to the risk.

"What if I have a look around for someone to target before we go in?" Sayen asked. "Don't forget my enhanced eyes allow me to see a lot of detail at a distance."

"We can't risk being spotted while you do that," Jas

replied, "and besides, whoever you see is going to change position before we get close enough to grab them. Krat. I don't know how we're going to manage it." She turned the problem over in her mind.

"Six minutes," Carl said. "I'm going to start her up in four. We've only got a thirty-second window. Jas, we don't have time to be hanging around chasing Shadows. If we delay, they'll figure out what's happening, and they'll get inside Sayen's place themselves."

"No," Sayen said. "We can't let that happen. Jas, how about we give up on catching a Shadow on our way in? We can try to do that once we're inside. There isn't a shortage of them in the area according to what my parents told me."

"I don't like it," said Jas. "They'll know we're there, and they'll be on the defensive. They might guess what we want to do because they know we kidnapped the minister. Your parents haven't attacked them, but they know *we* could. If we don't grab one when we have the opportunity, we'll lose the advantage of surprise."

"If we go in there with the shield down," Carl said, "they'll have clear shots at all of us."

Jas bit her lip. She couldn't decide what to do. For once, she wished someone else would take the lead. Her decisions didn't ever seem to be the right ones lately. The death of the minister they'd kidnapped weighed heavily on her. The woman had been incompetent at her job, it was true, but she hadn't deserved to die. Erielle had lost the use of her legs by trying to help them, and their friend, Ozment, whose truck they were in, had lost his life.

"Two minutes," Carl said.

"Krat it," said Jas. "Carl, tell me what you can see as we're driving in. If you can see a Shadow we might be able to capture, let me know, and I'll go after it. I guess it's the best we can do."

He started the engine. "Righto."

Jas took out her weapon and set it to stun as they pulled away from the curb.

Sayen's parents lived out of town on a huge estate. As well as a tall electrified fence surrounding the place, an invisible barrier formed a dome over the estate. When Jas and Carl had visited, Sayen had told them the barrier was to trap artificially cooled air, Jas guessed it had now been transformed into a force field to make the grounds impenetrable.

Their destination was easy to spot as an oasis of green in the surrounding dry, barren landscape. Jas had heard that the whole state had once been green and lush, but that rising global temperatures had changed the climate and dried up the rain.

Something had changed since her last visit. On the borders of the estate, opposite the front gates, construction of a large building was underway. This was how the Shadows were staking out Sayen's parents. They were building nearby, no doubt under the guise of a construction company. The shell of the first three floors were up already.

The truck was barreling down the road, only a minute from their destination. From a distance, the hard-hatted figures working inside the building were tiny and difficult to spot, but they didn't need to wait long before Shadows left the construction site and appeared on the road.

"Raising the shield," Carl said.

It slid smoothly into place, and the cab turned dark. A light blinked on. Jas was pushed back into her seat as Carl floored the gas. From all around came the sound of sizzling as the Shadows' lasers scored the shield.

"Nearly there," called Carl over the sound of the laser hits. The truck began to slow. If they entered Sayen's parent's estate at full speed, they would crash into the trees that lined the long, winding driveway.

"I see a Shadow you can get, Jas," exclaimed Carl. "On your side. Open your door and grab her."

They were all thrown forward as Carl braked hard. Jas flung open her door and put one foot down on the step, squinting in the glaring sunlight, trying to see the Shadow Carl had identified. The truck was still moving, and all she could see was a little girl, about eleven years old, holding a skipping rope.

"Get her," shouted Carl.

But Jas turned to him for confirmation that this was who he meant. *A child?* Laser fire hit the inside of the shield near her head, and she was nearly thrown from the truck as Carl pulled away violently. She retreated inside and slammed shut her door.

In another thirty seconds, the truck stopped. "We made it," Carl said. "We're inside."

They were safely behind the defenses of Sayen's home, but they had no Shadow.

2
____

The door that Jas had only recently slammed shut was wrenched open, and she was crushed beneath Sayen's mother as the woman leapt into the cab and climbed right over her. She grabbed her daughter, saying, "My baby. You're home. You're okay. I can't believe it. You're finally home."

"Mama, please," protested Sayen. "Calm down and get out of here. You're squashing Jas."

"I'm sorry, honey," she said. "I'm just so happy to see you again." She awkwardly clambered backward. Jas caught the woman's elbow as it was on its way into her face. She helped her as she climbed down from the cab onto the gravel of the driveway.

Jas also climbed down and moved out of the way so that the others had room to get out. Sayen's father embraced his daughter lovingly. The Lees' mansion was as Jas remembered it: massive and imposing.

Looking back in the direction they'd come, she saw figures peering through the estate's gates, keeping a respectful distance from the electrified metal. Smallest of the figures was the girl Carl had told her to capture.

He came over. "Why didn't you take her?"

"Do you really think she's a Shadow?"

"'Course she is. She's gotta be. Why else would a child be all the way out here in the middle of nowhere on a building site? Why would Shadows allow a human kid to hang out with them?"

"I don't know. I guess you're right. It just freaked me out for a moment. Krat. I missed our chance."

The Shadows were gazing at them and not even trying to pretend they were anything other than what they were. Even at a distance, she could see that their faces were expressionless. Up until then, she'd only seen rare glimpses of the natural state of the aliens. Most of the time they tried to mimic the humanity of the person they'd replaced. She supposed that they saw no need for pretenses now. A shiver ran down her spine. Not for the first time, she wondered who these mysterious aliens were, and what form they had before they copied human bodies to inhabit.

Behind her, Sayen's parents were urging them all to go inside, and she was happy to oblige. She'd had enough of Shadows for that day. For a lifetime, in fact.

"Wait, Mama, there's someone else," Sayen said. "Another friend. But she can't get out by herself. She's hurt. I have to help her." Sayen returned to the cab, where Erielle still lay, half hidden and unconscious.

"No, wait, honey," said her father. "Let Florence and Tyler do it." He motioned to the maid and butler who were standing in the doorway. The two android servants came down the steps, and at Sayen's instructions, they gently lifted Erielle out of the truck and carried her into the house.

With a final look at the watching figures of the Shadows, Jas followed the others inside.

At the sound of the door closing behind her, she relaxed for what felt like the first time in weeks. Whatever defenses Sayen's parents had against the Shadows, they seemed to be effective for the moment. There, they were as safe as they could be, even with the mysterious aliens sitting on the doorstep. It was odd, however, that this couple had military-style protection of their home. There hadn't been a war anywhere in the world in years, and the extent of their security went far beyond that needed to prevent burglaries or other home invasions. She wondered what it was that warranted the need.

"Oh, Sayen," exclaimed her mother, hugging her child again. "We thought you were dead. We thought the Shadows had caught you and murdered you."

"I know Mama. You told me so when I contacted you. Don't you remember? Now, where should Florence and Tyler put Erielle?"

"I think the red guest room would be best. That's nearest yours. I'll see what we can do for your friend. She looks very weak and dehydrated."

"Thank you, Mama. We all need food and something to drink. We haven't been able to buy anything for two days."

"That sounds awful," said Sayen's father. "Don't you worry. We'll see to it all. Florence will look after Erielle. Please, everyone, come through here and eat something. You must all be famished. And you two..." He turned to Jas and Carl. "Thank you for bringing my daughter home. I don't know how I'll ever repay you."

"You don't have anything to thank us for, Mr. Lee," said Carl. "Sayen saved our lives more than once."

"And mine," said Makey.

Sayen introduced the kid to her parents, and they went further into the house. Nothing was said for a while as the four ate and drank. No one could eat much after fasting for two days, but the water tasted like nectar to Jas.

"Where's Beau?" Sayen asked her parents.

Jas remembered the strange cat-dog hybrid that was Sayen's pet.

"I'm sorry," Sayen's mother replied. "We gave him away when we thought you weren't coming back. I couldn't bear to see him anymore. He reminded me of you."

Sayen sighed. "Okay. I'm going to check on Erielle." She put down her glass.

"She'll be fine," said Sayen's father. "You know Florence will give her the best care, just like the other maids used to give you when you were a little girl."

"I know, Daddy. I just can't rest until I see that she's okay." She got up and put down her napkin before leaving.

As Sayen closed the door behind her, Sayen's mother raised her eyebrows at her husband.

"If you don't mind my asking," said Mr. Lee. "Who is that woman, Erielle? Sayen didn't mention her when she called. She seems to have been seriously injured."

"She was," Jas replied. "She helped us kidnap the security minister—"

"That was you, was it?" said Mrs. Lee. "We saw the reports on the vidnews. She's been missing for days. Why would you do a thing like that? What's happened to the woman?"

"She's dead, I'm sorry to say. She got shot when we were attacked," said Jas ruefully. "I guess I should bring you up to speed. A lot's happened since we left you to go and rescue Sayen."

She and Carl narrated the events of their retrieving

Sayen from the Shadow facility in Antarctica, their first encounter with Erielle in the underworld neighborhood, and everything that had happened since. It took a while, and long before they'd finished, Sayen returned from checking on Erielle. She and Makey also contributed to their parts of the story. Sayen took over to explain how they'd stolen a Shadow scanner and how their friend, Ozment, had died.

As Sayen spoke, Jas went to the window, which looked out over the lawn of the estate. The green sward led down to a lake with flamingoes. The fence that marked the rear boundary far away was obscured by trees. She couldn't see it clearly. She wondered if Shadows were patrolling behind the estate as well as in front. As she watched, a dark shape appeared in the sky, flying closer. A heli. Not one of the small, domestic four-seaters, but a military vehicle. Her hand went to her mouth.

There was only one explanation for the heli being in the vicinity: the Shadows' reach had now extended into the Global Government Air Force. She was silently grateful that the aircraft hadn't turned up a couple of hours ago, or they would never have made it into the house. As always, they seemed to be only one step ahead of the encroaching Shadows.

"Krat," breathed Carl, who had joined her at the window while Sayen was finishing off their story.

"I know," said Jas.

The heli drew close. A beam of blinding light flashed out from it. About thirty meters above the ground, the beam encountered a barrier. The light split and zigzagged outward and down, outlining the shape of the force field that protected the estate.

"What the hell was that?" exclaimed Mr. Lee, leaping up

to look out the window. "A heli? Carleen, they've sent in the military. They certainly want y'all," he said to the others.

"It's the first time this has happened?" asked Jas. The heli had disappeared overhead, but it returned and swept a wide arc before approaching the house once more.

"Yes," Mr. Lee replied. "The Shadows have only been watching us up until now. They've never attempted an all-out attack." Another flash of intense light blazed from the aircraft and dissipated across the barrier.

"Will your force field withstand the charges?" Carl asked.

Mr. Lee rubbed his chin. "Yes—for a while."

Sayen's parents, Jas, and the others stood at the window watching the heli firing at the force field for a while, like it was a bizarre fireworks show. Eventually, the Shadows seemed to accept their efforts were pointless, and the heli flew off.

"Mama, Daddy," Sayen said as they returned to their seats. "Now it's your turn. What's been happening here? And how come you have all these defenses? You two have always been so secretive. I think it's high time you finally told me what it is you've been hiding from me and Phelan all these years."

"Oh, honey, I'm sorry. I know we haven't been open with you," said Mrs. Lee. "We were only trying to keep you and your brother safe."

"And I guess that's your reason for having a tracker put in my butt cheek," Sayen retorted, folding her arms.

"Well, as a matter of fact, it is," replied her mother. "We nearly lost you once. I wasn't going to risk losing you again."

"Mama," exclaimed Sayen, "how could you? That was an invasion of my privacy."

"I never checked up on you, I swear. I never once tried to

find out where you were. You're a grown woman, I know that. I didn't do it to snoop on you. It was only in case of an emergency. Aren't you grateful now that I did it?"

Sayen glared at her mother.

"Now, now," said her father. "What we did, we did, for better or worse. As it turned out, it was for the greater good in this case. But we can't fix it now. Sayen, sweetheart, you're right. I guess it is time that you know the truth about us." He sighed. "When you know, I hope you'll understand why we could never give you or Phelan the slightest hint about what we do. It was for your own safety as well as ours."

There was an uncomfortable pause as Sayen looked expectantly at her parents. Neither seemed to know how to begin. "Well? Are you going to tell me or not?"

"Perhaps it's better that I show you," said Mr. Lee. "All of you. If you would step this way."

He led them out of the room and up the wide, winding staircase of his palatial home. At the top of the stairs, sumptuous hallways opened on both sides, lined with deep plush carpet and lit by old-fashioned, ornate lamps. Jas wondered what Sayen's childhood had been like with this vast house as her play space. It was the kind of place you could get lost in but not really mind for a while.

Halfway down a corridor, they stopped at a closed door. A device of a kind Jas had never seen before protruded at head height from the wall—a security console of some kind. Mr. Lee put a hand to a panel and his face to a hole. He breathed into a tube while a scanner read his eyes. A small click signaled as the door opened. "I'll add y'all to the security database so that you can have a free run of the house while you're here," he said as they went inside.

The room looked like an ordinary office. Chairs and a desk, several interfaces, and knick-knacks were all Jas could see. Mr. Lee ignored all these and walked directly across the room to an area of blank wall. After pressing a raised panel, he stepped back as a section of the wall slid away to reveal an elevator. He spread his arm wide to invite them in.

Sayen gasped. "Daddy? Mama? What is this?"

"Step in here, sweetheart," said Mr. Lee, "and I'll show you. Come on, everyone. I think we can all fit."

"I'm going to check on your friend, honey," said Mrs. Lee. "Your daddy can explain everything."

They crowded into the small space. Mr. Lee gave a voice command, and they descended. The elevator stopped, and the doors opened. Spreading out in front of them, covering an area as wide and deep as the entire base of the Lees' home, was a workroom and laboratory rolled into one.

"Wow," said Makey.

3

Jas put an arm around Sayen, as the woman appeared to be about to faint.

"Daddy?" she asked weakly.

"I'm sorry, Sayen. I realize this must come as a terrible shock. I guess I'd best get this over with as quickly as I can. Please, everyone, come in and sit down." He led them into the massive room and pulled up a couple of laboratory stools next to a bench that was scattered with metal parts and tiny tools. As he left to find some more stools, Jas helped Sayen onto one of them. The normally chatty woman seemed unable to speak. She only gaped.

Uniform wooden benches occupied most of the vast space, but there were also fume cabinets and a wide range of machining tools, as well as many things Jas couldn't even recognize. On most of the benches were interfaces, and materials and instruments were spread about, as if work on something or things had been temporarily halted.

Mr. Lee brought over three more tall stools, and he and the others sat down. He laid a hand on Sayen's arm. "Sayen, this is what I could never let you or your brother know. I am breaking solemn oaths that I swore to uphold by telling you and your friends this. However, it looks like our government has been compromised, and to help save humankind, I must break my promises. My dear, your mother and I work for the Global Government in an absolutely top secret capacity."

"You...what do you mean? What is it you do?" Sayen asked, her voice almost childlike.

"I should probably have made up something to tell you both to stop you from wondering all this time, but I couldn't make up a believable alternative. Besides, neither your mother nor I could bring ourselves to lie to you. I know you and Phelan had a little game going on where you were trying to guess."

Jas wished the man would get to the point. They were under attack by hostile aliens. It was hardly the time for shilly shallying. But she supposed he'd been thinking about this for the last two or three decades.

"I guess you would call us inventors," he went on. "We design and create the prototypes of devices used for the purpose of espionage."

"You're spies?" exclaimed Sayen, her eyes wide.

"No, no, no," Mr. Lee replied. "We *make* the things used for spying. All kinds of things. The Government approaches us with a problem it needs to solve, such as how to gain access to some sensitive information, and we invent the appropriate device." He turned to Carl and Jas. "You remember I told you we were being shut out of governmental meetings? You probably thought we were involved in politics. We aren't, but we are privy to confidential government business. We have to be. If we don't know what's happening, we have no way of suggesting how we can help.

"About six months ago, we found we were not being invited to certain meetings that previously we had attended as a matter of course. We also received many invitations to leave our estate. The reasons we were given for our requested departure were weak. This was highly unusual. Our colleagues and acquaintances are aware of our general reclusiveness, which is partly natural and partly precautionary. It would be a serious blow to the Government if it were to lose our services. Its enemies would love to have the information we hold. Why would it invite us to expose ourselves to danger?"

He turned to his daughter. "Sayen, you and Phelan were also at risk. If anyone had taken you from us, we would have done anything to get you back, and enemies of the Government knew that. We have been excessively protective of you both, I admit. I hope you understand why now."

Sayen got up and threw her arms around her father. "Daddy, I'm so sorry. I'm sorry I got mad at you and Mama."

Jas glanced at Carl. He had his head down. She guessed he was probably thinking of his missing parents. She leaned over and gave his arm a squeeze. He looked up and smiled at her sadly.

"This place is sneck," said Makey. "Can I have a look around?"

"No, I'm afraid not," replied Mr. Lee. "Perhaps one day I'll show you some things, but not now. Let's head back up to my office, where we can look at the problem at hand."

They filed once more into the elevator, and he returned them to the room with the interfaces.

He pressed a hand on a wall screen, and it blinked on, displaying a chart. After several swipes of lines and figures, Mr. Lee nodded. "As I thought. They've cut us off entirely now. First, we lost our direct comm to governmental colleagues. A temporary fault, we were told. Then we lost contact with all out-of-state connections. We could send and receive local comms only. Now, everything's gone."

"Does it matter, though?" Jas asked. "We're surrounded by Shadows. All we have to do is capture one, scan it to check that it is what we think it is, then contact the Transgalactic Council. That's why we're here."

"Contact the Council?" asked Mr. Lee, his eyebrows raised. "You think we didn't think of that? It was the first thing we tried after you and Carl set off to retrieve Sayen. Just before you arrived, we'd sent a packet to our son's starship to tell him his sister was missing. Then after you left, we tried to contact the Transgalactic Council to inform them of, well, everything you'd told us—about the Shadows and so on, but our deep space comm link was gone. It's been gone all this time."

"What?" exclaimed Jas. "We're kratted then. If we can't contact the Council, Earth doesn't have a hope. We need their help. The Shadows are moving fast. We already don't have the numbers to stop them on our own."

"Wait a moment before you give up," said Mr. Lee. "Listen. I despaired too when I realized what the Shadows had done, but I've been working on the problem since then. You saw that building when you came in? That's where they're housing the suppressor that's preventing deep space comms in and out of here. I've been trying to figure out a way to get inside the building and destroy the machine, but I'm seventy years old and hardly cut out for climbing around in the dark. Then I saw your truck..."

Carl looked up. His face had lost its gloomy look. "Now that's an idea. You mean we could just drive right in there and smash this suppressor down?"

"Something along those lines."

"I'll do it," said Carl.

"Hold on," Jas said. "Aren't you forgetting something? We need a Shadow to show them as proof first before you go smashing anything."

"Oh, yeah," said Carl. "Well, that shouldn't be too hard. It isn't like they're difficult to spot around here."

"It isn't going to be that easy," Jas replied. "They know we're here now, and we don't exactly have a history of friendliness toward them. They're going to be expecting us to do something. They'll be watching. The minute anyone steps out, they'll be on us."

"Shame you didn't get that Shadow girl while you could," Makey said.

"Hey, it wasn't easy," Jas protested.

"You mean a young girl with a skipping rope?" Mr. Lee asked.

"Yeah," Carl replied. "She looks about ten or eleven."

"I know her. She's out there all the time. I think they're trying to tempt us to go and talk to her. They seem to understand that humans are predisposed to be friendly toward children."

"Have you ever spoken to her?" Jas asked.

"Goodness no," replied Mr. Lee.

"Good call, Daddy," Sayen said. "I saw her too. She gives me the creeps. She'd probably shoot you the minute you got in range."

"She can't shoot us through the force field," replied her father, "but I don't want to hear whatever it is that thing has to say. Which reminds me, I must check on how the force field's holding up against that heli attack." He swiped and pressed the screen, bringing up an image of the estate grounds. Two helis were there now, and the sky was alive with their onslaught. Overlaid on the image were a set of fluctuating graphs.

"We're good for the moment," said Mr. Lee, "but I hope they don't have much more to throw at us. The generators can only provide a finite amount of energy."

"The sooner we catch a Shadow and take out that suppressor, the better," said Jas.

"Yes, but what then?" Sayen asked. "I've been thinking, if we do get a packet through to the Council, and they take notice, it isn't like they'll be able to come here and rescue us right away. We're going to be at the Shadows' mercy until help arrives."

There was a pause. Jas, like almost everyone else it seemed, hadn't considered what would happen after they achieved their goal. The Shadows knew they were there. They knew that the humans they had trapped were trying to wreck their plans. The aliens weren't going to give up until they were all dead and had their own Shadow clones as replacements.

Mrs. Lee stuck her head around the door. "Sayen, your friend's awake, and she's asking for you."

4

———

Sayen had always liked the red guest room the best, and if her mother hadn't suggested putting Erielle in there, she would have asked for it. The room was named for its deep red velvet curtains and rug, which contrasted beautifully with deep cream walls and furniture. There was also an amazing view over the gardens at the rear of the house and the distant hills, where the sun rose in the mornings. As a little girl, Sayen had taken her dolls in there to play and had spent many happy hours pretending that it was a royal court, and that the king and queen were receiving visitors.

It was a surprise to her to see the sour look on Erielle's face. The older woman was sitting up in the sumptuous double bed, looking much better than she had when they'd arrived. She was clean and wearing the sleepwear that Sayen's parents kept for guests. Her hair, which she normally kept close-cropped or even shaved, had begun to grow out in salt-and-pepper shades, and her gaunt face and frame showed the evidence of her many ordeals. But her inner strength and passion hadn't faded. Without her needing to say a word, Sayen could tell the woman's feelings were on fire.

She sat on the edge of the bed and took Erielle's hand. "Is something wrong?" she asked, almost timidly.

"So this is your parents' place?" her lover replied. "From the modding and enhancement you've received, I knew they had money. That was obvious. Maybe I was naive, but I never imagined quite *how much*."

Erielle's tone was harsh. Sayen felt like the woman expected her to apologize for her parents' wealth, as if it were wrong or somehow her fault. She looked down into her lap. "I thought you'd like it here. I thought it would be somewhere that you could rest and get better. And maybe with time, you might change your mind about your legs. My parents would—"

"Don't you dare," spat Erielle, raising a finger in warning. "Don't you dare say it. I am certainly *not* taking your parents' money to get my legs fixed. If I ever get them fixed."

Sayen let go of her hand. She wondered what had happened to that dynamic, ardent, loving woman she'd gotten to know only a couple of weeks before. Now, Erielle seemed full of nothing more than pain, anger, and hate. After all the arguments they'd had about getting her the treatment she needed to take away her pain and allow her to walk again, which the woman stubbornly refused to consider, Sayen could hardly bear being around her anymore.

She got up and went to the window. She looked out over the green lawns. The helis had disappeared for the moment. On the other side of the house, the sun was going down, and a deep shadow spread across the grass.

Sayen turned to face her lover. "Is it really so bad, Erielle? My parents have worked hard for everything they have. It isn't like they inherited their money. Every penny they have, they earned. I just found out that due to what they do, they were—are—also in a lot of danger. My brother and I too. I get that other people aren't so well off, but it isn't like that's my parents' fault. My mama and daddy aren't undeserving. They help keep the world safe, and they donate a lot of money to charity. They fund plenty of projects in poorer countries."

"You think it's generous of them to give away a portion of their billions?" asked Erielle. "Tell me, Sayen, what did you or anyone in your family go without so that they could donate that money? Did you suffer at all? Did you miss out? I'm guessing that, no, you did not. So what makes your parents' generosity so noble? Do you have any idea how many people your parents could help if they gave everything they have? Do you know how much good they could do? But they don't, do they? When you give what you can easily afford, it means nothing. Those charity projects are just an afterthought to your folks. No, instead of helping someone who desperately needs it, they'd rather have kratting *flamingoes* in their lake."

Sayen's face burned. No one had ever spoken to her like that about her parents and their money. Whenever she'd let it slip that her family was very wealthy, most people were mildly jealous, or they would ask her about what it was like growing up in luxury. No one had ever made her feel ashamed of something she had no control over, or embarrassed about the two people she loved the most in the world, and who had never shown her anything but their utter devotion.

She balled her fists. "And what if Mama and Daddy gave everything away, as if they *should*? What a joke that would be. You and your underworlder friends would only spend it on kratom, or booze, or myth. My parents worked hard. They used their brains. They made a *difference*. What the krat have you ever done except run away from your job and your responsibilities? You were a trained surgeon, and you gave it all up to lead a bunch of losers and misfits in their stupid, pointless, posturing, pathetic waste of time they have the arrogance to call their lives.

"Do you know what happened after you went missing, Erielle? I never told you. You were out of it most of the time, and I didn't want to upset you. But it took less than a day of your absence before everything you'd built up for so many years started to fall apart. All those people you'd led and cared for and nurtured? They didn't give a krat about you. *We* were the ones who wanted to go out and find you. It was Jas and Ozment who scoured the streets hoping to stumble across you. All the rest of your misborn underworlder friends didn't give a krat. All they cared about was where their next run was coming from. So I'm not going to apologize because my parents are rich. They have what they deserve, and so do you underworlders."

She stormed across the room, barely taking in Erielle's look of shock. She flung open the door and nearly walked directly into Jas, who was outside. With a snort of frustration, she side-stepped the Martian and stalked away.

Jas caught up to her in a few strides. "Er...things not going so well between you and Erielle?"

"Hmpf. I've had it with her, Jas. I don't know what I ever saw in her. I don't think I ever met anyone so pigheaded, arrogant, or holier-than-thou. I mean, who does she think she is, criticizing the only place where she's safe and can recover? You'd think she'd be just a little grateful—just the tiniest bit thankful that we had this place to escape to. But no. It isn't *humble* enough for her.

Erielle's too good for my parents' home, where they've welcomed her as a guest. She needs a hovel to languish and die in just so she can feel *comfortable*. So her fine feelings of *equality* aren't offended."

Jas sighed and put an arm around her. "I don't get what you mean," she said with a small smile. "Stop beating around the bush and tell me how you really feel."

Sayen gave a snort of laughter. A little of her anger dissipated. "Thanks, Jas. I needed that. I guess I'm overreacting a little. Erielle said some ugly things about my parents and my home, but she's still not fully recovered, and she's in a lot of pain. I shouldn't forget that."

"Yeah," Jas said, "with Erielle's beliefs, it would be hard for her to wrap her head around a place like this. I had a little trouble myself when I first saw it, and I don't ever think about things like money or who has what. It's a little hard to take in."

"Maybe I'll go and see her again later," said Sayen. "When I've had a chance to cool down. I might apologize for some of the things I said. I don't want to be her enemy. I like her and I want to be her friend. But, you know, Jas, I don't think we'll ever be more than that again. We're just too incompatible." She looked up at her friend and smiled wistfully. "Sorry, my love life isn't your concern. What are you doing here? Did you want to see me about something?"

"I don't mind hearing about your problems, Sayen, but I'm probably not a good person to talk to. I'm not great at that kind of thing myself. Anyway, I came to tell you what we decided. You and I are going to capture one of the Shadows. Carl and Makey are going to figure out a way to take down the suppressor that's preventing the deep space comms. But we need to do our job before the guys can do theirs. We'll use the scanner to make sure we really have a

Shadow. Then your parents will contact the Transgalactic Council and show them the evidence."

"And then what happens?"

Jas sighed. "I have no idea. But we'll do our part. We'll have tried at least. After that, it'll be up to more important people than us to figure out how to defeat the Shadows."

"The people more important than us haven't done such a great job so far."

"You're not wrong, but there's still hope. It sounds like your parents are respected and have a lot of important connections. The Council will listen to them. They'll have to help Earth if they want to stop the Shadows from spreading across the galaxy. I just hope there are enough people left to defeat the invasion here."

"Me too. So what are we doing? How are we going to capture a Shadow?"

"Now that we have your mom and dad's workshop at our disposal, I don't think it's going to be too difficult. What we want to do is find a Shadow when it's on its own, stun it, and bring it in here. We want to avoid a gunfight with the others if we can. We don't want to take more risks than we have to. We've been burned enough."

"I'm all for that. My skin recovers quickly from a laser burn, but it sure as hell hurts when it happens. So how are we going to know when a Shadow is on its own?"

"Your dad says he has something that will help."

5

The fennec fox looked like it was asleep, except for the fact that it wasn't breathing. Makey reached out and stroked its fur, which was about the finest, softest thing he'd ever felt. The animal was cold to the touch. This wasn't surprising because it wasn't real, though he was having a hard time believing it.

"It's so lifelike," he said to Mr. Lee, who was adjusting controls on an interface screen.

"Hmmm," replied the man, his head down as he concentrated on what he was doing. "That's the idea. If it's spotted, it should pass for the real thing, at a cursory glance anyway."

Makey, Sayen, and Jas were in the basement laboratory with Sayen's father, gathered around the animal he'd built as a surveillance device.

"Wouldn't it be better to use a mosquito or something a similar size?" asked Sayen. "The fox is small, but it wouldn't be that hard to spot and destroy if someone suspected what it was."

"It isn't that easy to spot in this landscape. It's very well camouflaged. Fennec foxes are notoriously difficult for predators other than man to catch. They're virtually invisible against a desert background, and they're fast and nimble. It was the first animal that sprung to mind when I first thought of creating something to spy on the Shadows around us. I've used it successfully three times now. That was how I first located the suppressor within that building they're constructing."

"But wouldn't a mosquito be more maneuverable?" Sayen persisted. "I mean, at the first sign of trouble, it could fly away."

"You're right, sweetheart, but a mosquito's too small. Let me tell you how this thing works, and then you'll understand. A mosquito is fine and dandy for standard surveillance. In fact, I have a number of them just over there that I designed and made myself. But even with the latest in storage capacity, it isn't large enough. Now an animal like this is about the right size. Only a small part of this fox is given over to its locomotion, sensory, and transmitting equipment—of course, there's no need to include the other parts of the natural animal, such as its digestive system—the rest of it is given over to housing the operator's consciousness."

"What?" exclaimed Jas. "The person operating it...you mean it holds their mind? They embody this thing?"

"That's right. A direct mind connection with a surveillance device is far more effective than operating one at a distance. Anyone can do it, providing I link them up to its system. The capacity remaining aside from the space required for the other necessary components is roughly the size of a human brain. It would be an abomination to put a real brain in there, of course, but the material we use mimics the complexity of neurons and other cells that make up the human brain. Not perfectly. We haven't managed to achieve that yet. But perfection isn't necessary. It isn't like anyone's going to live in there."

Makey could hardly believe his ears. Since arriving on Earth, he'd been turned speechless more than once at the amazing things he'd encountered—things that he'd never even imagined while growing up on Dawn. But if he understood Mr. Lee correctly, this latest object was almost beyond belief. The man seemed to be saying that someone could transfer their mind to the animal and operate it from the inside, as if that person were the animal itself.

"What happens to the person's body while their mind is in the animal?" he asked.

"Nothing at all. All human functions necessary to life continue as before—heartbeat, lung function, metabolism, none of these requires the mind to work. Sadly, we used to see that in previous generations when people would suffer brain death but their bodies would continue to live on as if nothing had happened. Thankfully, no one has to suffer that indignity any longer."

"I meant what happens in the operator's mind? Can you be in the animal and aware of your body at the same time?" Makey asked.

"No, that would be too disorienting I think. I've set up the system so that isn't possible. Once you're in the fox, you're only aware of everything from its perspective. You see through its eyes, listen through its considerable ears, and feel through its fur and mouth. Of course, whatever the fox sees and hears, etcetera, is also displayed on this screen and recorded."

"And how do you get out of it again?" asked Makey.

Mr. Lee smiled. "I believe we have a budding scientist in our midst. When we have more time, I will explain to you exactly how to operate the device and how it works, though you'd probably have to study several degree-level courses to understand. It was Sayen's mother who programmed the consciousness transference. I have to admit I don't understand it too well myself. Suffice to say, the operator learns a mental sequence that triggers the return to their body. With luck, that should only happen when the device has returned. I wouldn't like to lose it in the field. It would take me days to make another."

Makey had a horrible feeling that, from what Mr. Lee was saying, *he* wasn't going to be the one operating the fox. His heart sank. He didn't think he'd ever wanted anything so much in his whole life, except maybe that his sister and mam could return from the dead.

Mr. Lee read his expression. "When this is all over, Makey, not only will I explain how to operate this fox, I will allow you to do so."

"Sneck," Makey exclaimed. "Thanks."

"But for now," Jas said, "I believe that Carl will want to talk to you about destroying that suppressor."

"Awww," Makey whined, "but that isn't until after you and Sayen have caught a Shadow. That isn't for ages. I'd rather stay here and watch someone transfer their mind to that fox."

"Makey," said Jas in that voice that meant she didn't want to have to say anything else.

"Oh, okay. I'm going." He left them and went up in the elevator. He found Carl outside the front of the house, where he was inspecting the truck.

Though it was a tough vehicle, it had taken plenty of damage when Ozment had driven it through the perimeter fence and warehouse wall at the spaceport. The grill was buckled, and the top of the cab was crumpled. Black streaks ran down the sides from the heli attack.

"She's a beauty, eh?" Carl asked. "Don't you think?"

"Er," was all Makey could think to reply.

It didn't matter. The Australian was lost in his admiration of the vehicle. "Never had a chance to really look at her till now. I can remember trucks like this from when I was a kid. Big, ten-wheeled monsters with tires bigger than me. I used to dream of driving one across the Nullabor. Nothing around me but the desert and the sea. Nothing above but the sky. For hundreds and hundreds of kilometers. That'd be an experience. Not, mind you," he said, waggling a finger at Makey, "that it would beat flying. Nothing beats that. Still, it'd be great, wouldn't it?"

"I suppose so. Um, Jas sent me up here to talk to you about destroying the suppressor."

Carl's eyes and mind were still on the truck. He had his hands on his hips, and he was nodding thoughtfully at some scenario playing in his head. After a moment of silence, Makey's words seemed to register. "Did you say something, mate? Oh, yeah, destroying the suppressor. Yeah. That's our job. Right." He pulled open the driver's side door. "Hop in."

"Huh?" said Makey. "That's your side."

"Oh no. You'll be driving. I've got to get up on top."

"What?" Makey exclaimed. "You mean you're going to sit where Ozment died?"

"Someone has to. The Shadows have got two helis. The minute we start this thing up, they'll be onto us. We won't have long before they figure out what we're going to do and try to take us out. Before they figure out what we're doing, maybe. If we've got no defense, we'll be sitting ducks."

"Then I'll do it. I'll go up there," said Makey. "I'm an ace shot. Jas said so."

"No. No way. You're too young. Jas won't hear of it, and I agree with her."

Makey clenched his jaw. He wished they would all stop treating him like a kid. "I'm not too young. I'm not allowed to do anything. It's like you all don't want me to grow up."

"It isn't that. Kid, we don't let you do stuff *because* we want you to grow up. We want you to have the chance."

Makey sighed. The man only wanted to look out for him. "Okay. Are you going to teach me how to drive?"

"That's right. Come on." They climbed up into the cab, and Carl began showing him the different controls and telling him what they did.

"You know," Carl said, "I used to imagine teaching my kid to drive one day. Keep the old skills going, you know. I never thought I'd be teaching a seventeen-year-old colony pup. Still, you'll do. Now, usually it'd be hard to find a place for you to practice driving a vehicle this size, but we're lucky. We've got acres of parkland to drive around in. We'll take her round the back of the house."

"Do you think Sayen's parents are going to mind us ruining their lawn?"

"Right now," Carl said as a heli rose up from beyond the half-finished building at the end of the driveway, "I think that's the least of their worries."

6

Jas was inside the fennec fox. Wrong. She *was* the fox. The figures of Sayen and Mr. Lee were impossibly high above her, almost unrecognizable from her new perspective. To her left, she could see her own legs, as her body, which she'd temporarily left, sprawled unconscious in a reclining chair.

"How do you feel, Jas?" asked Mr. Lee, peering down at her. His voice was almost painful in her super-sensitive ears. "As I explained, you aren't able to speak, so nod if you're okay."

Jas tried to nod, and the fox's head obeyed her thoughts. The world moved up and down in response. She staggered, feeling extremely disoriented. If she'd had a stomach, she would have been sick.

"It'll take you a few minutes to accustom yourself to the experience," Mr. Lee said. "Take your time. Walk around a little."

"I still think *I* should be the one doing this," said Sayen.

"And I still think that we need your enhanced powers right here in case of an attack," replied her father.

Jas took a tentative step on her right front paw. Which leg came next? One of her back legs, probably, but which one? She tried to move her right rear leg and wobbled dangerously. That wasn't right. She quickly brought her left front leg forward to compensate. But then her right rear leg was in the wrong place. She returned all four legs to their starting points. This needed some figuring out.

Meanwhile, her mind was becoming aware of a rich range of sensations. The most noticeable were the signals coming from her nose. She smelled odors she could never have believed possible before. And so many of them. She smelled the sour, metallic aroma of the dust on the floor. The scents of Sayen and her father were heavy in the air. They smelled different from each other, but there were similarities that told Jas the two were related.

Her hearing was also turned up to a much higher capacity. She could hear the three humans in the room breathing and the sounds of their intestines moving, squeezing food and gas along. Somewhere, a fly was trapped in a web, and a spider was picking its way toward its victim.

Vibrations from the floor through her paws told her that Ozment's truck had started up outside. She could even detect the movement of air currents against the highly sensitive hairs inside her ears.

She tried to move her legs again. After putting her right front paw forward, she followed the movement with her left rear paw, then repeated the action with the legs on the opposite sides. That worked much better.

"Well done, Jas," Sayen said. "You're getting it."

Soon, she was running around the laboratory. Embodying a surveillance device in the shape of a small animal was fun, she decided. She wished she had more time to explore this new experience, but they couldn't waste a moment in capturing a Shadow. She nudged Mr. Lee's leg with her nose.

"You're ready?" he asked. "Good. Follow me."

He took her up in the elevator to the first floor and out into the conservatory full of orchids Jas'sd seen on her first visit. Mrs. Lee was there. She was with the maid, Florence. The android's chest was open, and Sayen's mother had both hands inside. She looked over her shoulder as her husband and daughter and a small, pale brown fox appeared.

"Jas, you seem to be doing fine," the woman said. "Good luck. Don't forget the sequence for returning to your own body when you get back. Or if things get too hairy out there, activate the sequence and just leave the fox behind. We can always make another one. We can't make another Jas."

Jas wished she could thank her.

Mr. Lee opened the doors that led outside to the huge green lawn. Dusk was falling. "I'm going to show you a tiny place in the force field where you can slip through," he said. "It's too small for any human, even that creepy little Shadow girl. But you can fit it. You must come back the same way, and preferably unseen, though I can seal the spot if Shadows follow you and try to break through."

Jas, Mr. Lee, and Sayen walked across the lawn toward the woods that bordered the furthest reaches of the Lees' estate. The Shadow-controlled helis had stopped attacking for the moment. Jas wondered if they had only been testing the strength of the force field and were preparing themselves for a serious assault. She estimated they had a day or maybe two at most to carry out their plans. The Shadows were moving fast. It would be only a short time before they gathered the firepower to breach the Lees' defenses. Either that or they would have replaced enough of the population with Shadows to do away with the need for subterfuge.

Her paws crunched on the dry leaf mold beneath the trees as they entered the woods. The trees stretched only fifty meters wide. They arrived at the thick-wired fence that stood between the verdant private gardens and the surrounding desert landscape. Jas searched for watching Shadows, but there were none. It was a good sign. The aliens didn't seem to have the numbers to surround the place—yet. Mr. Lee led them along the fence to an area that didn't appear to be any different from the rest. Jas wondered how she would find it again when she returned from spying on the Shadows.

Mr. Lee took a pair of glasses out of his pocket. After putting them on, he scanned the fence where it met the ground.

"We have a hidden gate in this fence back near the house, but I'd have to turn off the electricity for you to open it. At this spot, you can return whenever you're ready. We don't have to prearrange a time."

"Couldn't the Shadows just dig under the fence, Daddy?" Sayen asked.

"They could try," he replied, "but it goes ten meters deep and it's electrified all the way down, though the under-ground part is insulated in plastic. Ah, here it is." He took a bottle from his jacket pocket, opened it, and shook a few drops of a clear liquid on the ground next to the fence wires. "Can you smell that, Jas?"

She trotted over and sniffed the ground. The stench was so powerful it made her reel backward. She gave a huge sneeze and shook her head.

Mr. Lee laughed. "I'm sorry. I made the pheromone a little strong, but it works. Humans can't register the scent, and I'm guessing that Shadow humans can't either. Only you will be able to find it, Jas. When you return, sniff along the border until you smell it, then pass through where the odor is strongest."

"But she can't," Sayen said. "Even a small animal can't fit through the gaps in the wires."

"There is no fence just there. Use these." He passed Sayen his glasses. "It's an optical illusion."

"Oh yes," she exclaimed. "I can see it. A small gap."

"Ordinarily," Mr. Lee said, "we would have only the electrified fence protecting the grounds and the air barrier to seal in the cool air. I've turned the air barrier into a force field that extends all the way to the ground, but left this tiny entrance open. However, Jas, take care not to touch the fence. It's still electrified."

Easy for you to say, thought Jas. *You can see the hole.* To her, the fence looked complete. She had only the pheromone that Mr. Lee had sprinkled and his word to rely on. Unfortunately, she couldn't tell him that.

Looking down at her from his great height, the man seemed to guess her concerns. "There's plenty of room for you. You won't be in any danger of electrocution providing you follow your nose, so to speak."

Jas approached the stink again and got ready to walk through the apparently solid wires. She took a final look at Sayen and Mr. Lee. Sayen's hand hesitated, as if she were resisting an urge to give her a pat.

"Good luck, Jas," she said.

"Yes, good luck," said Mr. Lee. "We'll return to the lab and check your progress on the screen. Don't forget, you can activate the sequence to return to your body at any time. It's preferable that you return in the device, of course. It would take me longer than we have to make another one."

He was right. Time was of the essence. Night was falling. She had to go and find a Shadow for them to capture.

She set her nose toward the fence where the ground smelled strongest and went forward. As she was about to touch the wires, they seemed to suddenly melt away. In a moment, she was through and outside, standing on desert dirt instead of leaf litter. The ground was still hot from the day's sun, though the fur on her paws was doing a great job of protecting her from the worst of it.

Sniffing the air, she detected little but dry vegetation in the vicinity, and she could hear nothing but the warm wind passing over the dusty ground. She would have to walk around the estate to the front to find the Shadows.

7

Makey turned the truck's steering wheel and followed the driveway as it led around the Lees' mansion to the gardens at the back. Driving the vehicle was a lot easier than he'd thought it would be. Not for the first time, he wondered why his Da and the Dawntowners thought that mechanical things were so evil. This truck didn't give off the bad gases he'd heard them talk about, which had polluted the air and made the global temperatures rise. It ran on electricity. The Lees had charged up the nearly dead battery soon after he and the others arrived.

Though he didn't like the truck as much as Carl did, he couldn't see anything bad about it. It was certainly going to be useful for taking out that suppressor Mr. Lee had told them about.

He pressed the brake. They'd run out of paved roadway. If they went any farther, they would be driving on grass.

"What's up?" Carl asked from the passenger seat. "You're doing great."

"Are you sure it's okay for us to do this?"

"Makey, if we don't drive this truck into that suppressor and destroy it, we're all gonna die. Do you think Sayen's parents would prefer a nice lawn over not dying? Geez, mate. Look, here's Mr. Lee. You can ask him for yourself."

Mr. Lee and Sayen were crossing the grass on their way back to the house. Carl lowered his window and called out to them, "Hey, Mr. Lee, is it all right if Makey gets some driving practice in on your lawn?"

"Go ahead," said Mr. Lee, "but first, let me show you something."

Makey turned off the engine, and they got out of the truck. They went inside and upstairs with Mr. Lee to his office, where he brought up an image on the large interface on his office wall. It was a mass of wave patterns, all flowing across the screen.

"Our sensors are picking these up. They're what's preventing us from sending a deep space packet to our contact at the Transgalactic Council. I'll show you what I've found." He swiped the screen, and it turned black. With a finger, he drew a sketch of an aerial view of the Shadows' building. "The suppressor is here." He drew an X at the bottom left corner. "That's the side facing away from us."

"Not next to the road, the other side?" Carl asked.

"That's right. If you crash the truck into this corner, you should destroy the machine."

"Won't that destroy the truck, too?" Makey asked. They were talking about driving into solid brick, not the corrugated metal wall they'd encountered at the spaceport.

"Yeah, I'd say so," Carl replied. "She's a tough old thing, but I don't think she'll survive that. More's the shame."

"And then what happens?" Makey asked.

"We fight our way out," said Carl, "or something. Don't

worry, we'll figure it out. The most important thing is to take out that suppressor."

Makey swallowed. Suddenly, learning to drive the truck seemed like a piece of cake. He'd thought they'd reached some kind of safety at Sayen's parents' home, but of course that had been stupid. No one was safe anymore. It didn't matter, he decided. He would stop the Shadows, whatever it took, in memory of Mam and Neeve.

"You all right, mate?" Carl asked.

"Yeah, I'm fine. You were saying we have to drive the truck through here?" Makey pointed to the sketch on the screen. "Then I reckon we should come off the road where it bends. What do you think, Carl?"

"I think you're right." Carl put a hand on his shoulder. "Yeah, you're right. That gives us the best angle. Well done."

Makey smiled and felt a warm glow at the older man's words. Finally, someone was treating him like an adult. If only he had a dad a bit more like Carl or Mr. Lee.

"Do you really think you can do it?" Mr. Lee said. "You realize you'll be under aerial attack?"

"I thought about that," Carl replied. "Our friend, Ozment, built some kind of missile launcher into the roof of the truck. You can't see it from the ground. Poor fella died up there."

Mr. Lee's eyebrows rose. "You must show me. Maybe I can improve it for you."

They returned downstairs, and Mr. Lee took them into the conservatory, where his wife was still working on the android. "Carleen, would you come with us? I think you could lend us a hand with something."

They all passed through the conservatory doors and into the garden, where the massive, battle-scarred truck now blocked the view of the lawn, lake, and trees. Night lay over the estate, and the stars were coming out. Carl took them into the truck cabin and pointed out the homemade tunnel that led to the roof.

While Mr. Lee returned to the house for flashlights. Carl went up the tunnel, followed by Mrs. Lee. Carl called down to Makey, telling him not to join them because there wasn't room for more than two people, so he sat in the cab, feeling a little left out again and wondering what the others were doing.

Bobbing lights coming from the house attracted his attention. Mr. Lee had returned with an android servant. Both were carrying flashlights and ladders.

"Would you like to have a look too, son?" he asked as he placed a ladder against the side of the truck. Makey didn't need to be asked twice. He was out of the cab and up the ladder in a flash, while the android held it steady.

At the top, he found he was looking down into a pit sunk into the truck's roof. The top edge was level with the rest of the roof, so unless you were looking at it from a higher point, you wouldn't know the pit existed. Carl and Mrs. Lee were in there examining a large weapon. Makey had no idea what it was, but it looked powerful. Mr. Lee joined him at the top of a second ladder and shone a flashlight into the pit. The beams lit up the operator's chair that was next to the weapon. The seat was stained darkly with what Makey realized had to be Ozment's blood. And now Carl was going to be in the exact same position.

"Craven," Mrs. Lee said, "do you think you could make some kind of shield to fit over this thing? It won't withstand a single direct hit as it is."

"I sure can," he replied. "I can do it overnight. I'm thinking that tungsten/graphene alloy. I have a few sheets left. And I can reinforce the truck walls. What do you think?"

"Sounds fine. And I'll work on upgrading this for maximum firepower and automatic targeting. Don't you worry, sugar," she said to Carl. "Any of those helis comes within spitting distance of this truck, you'll be taking them out of the sky quicker than you can blink at them."

"Thanks, Mr. and Mrs. Lee," Carl said. "I appreciate it."

"No need to thank us," said Mr. Lee. "We're all in this together. Isn't that right, son?" He addressed his question to Makey.

"Yes, sir, that's right."

The blackness of the night was split by a dazzling burst of light. The air was filled with a sizzling, crackling noise. Makey was momentarily blinded. The beam that had struck was far more powerful than the ones the Shadow helis had fired earlier.

"What the hell was that?" Carl asked.

"Looks like the Shadows are back, and they've upgraded," said Mr. Lee.

"What was it, Craven?" Mrs. Lee asked. "Do you know?"

"Some kind of pulse cannon, I guess."

"How long can the force field take it?" she asked.

"We should make it through the night. I wonder if they've guessed our energy is from solar power, and that's why they waited until nighttime to attack?"

"Lord knows," Mrs. Lee said. "I hope you're right and that we make it until dawn. There's nothing much we can do anyway. Might as well keep busy getting this ready. Can you lend us a hand, son?" she asked Makey. "We're going to need all the help we can get if we're going to finish by morning."

"Of course I can," he replied.

8

The cool night air chilled Jas's nose and the tips of her ears, but the failing light didn't affect her vision. If anything, things seemed to become clearer and sharper. The desert was alive with sound as the nocturnal creatures were waking up and leaving the places they hid from the hot sun during the day.

She ran alongside the security fence, keeping a good distance from its electrified wires. It wasn't long before she reached the road. The pavement was deserted. She kept low as she scooted across, a fleeting shadow herself in the deep twilight. Silently, she made her way down the bank and across the distance that separated her from the Shadow's construction site.

All she had to do was to find a likely Shadow to snatch. One of the aliens alone in a place it probably wouldn't leave for a while, such as asleep in bed. Then she could return to the Lees' home and her own body, and she and Sayen could slip out, take the Shadow, and bring it back as quickly and quietly as possible.

When they had the Shadow scanner readout, everything would be ready to send to the Council.

The dark-windowed building was drawing nearer as she trotted along, wondering what she would find inside. She wondered if the Shadows continued regular human lives when they lived in their replicated bodies, or if they behaved according to their alien minds.

Not panting with exertion after the long run felt weird. The side of the building loomed up. Jas slipped around the back, hoping to find a rear entrance. There was none, and though the windows were only frames without any glass, they were much too high for her to reach. She would have to enter at the front.

A few Shadows were hanging around outside as if waiting for something. None of them noticed her scurry behind them and into the cooler interior of the building.

On the first floor at least, the Shadows had constructed rooms with ceilings. They were bare and dusty. Where did they eat and sleep, she wondered. Surely their bodies had the same requirements as those of the humans they'd copied?

Jas ran silently down a corridor. She turned one corner, and then another. Still, she met no Shadows. What lay around the third corner made her stop in her tracks. A terrifyingly familiar, dark gray shape seemed to rear up. It was a hexagonal block, and in its center was a hexagonal hole. A Shadow trap. They'd built a trap within the building.

She froze in the center of the corridor, her shock making her momentarily unwary of the danger of being seen. Why had the Shadows constructed one of their traps out in the middle of nowhere? The Lees lived kilometers from their nearest neighbors. Had the aliens gone to all that trouble just to replicate Sayen's parents, and maybe herself and her friends? It seemed like overkill.

Her super-sensitive ears swiveled backward as a faint noise came from behind her. It was the sound of voices, as well as car doors slamming. Had more Shadows arrived, or...? Her heart sank as she viewed the trap's gaping hole. Was it some human victims? Were the Shadows supplementing their numbers at the site by bringing in people to replicate?

Her ears twitched. The voices were drawing nearer, and the floor vibrated faintly with many footsteps. She glanced left and right. The corridor was bare, with nowhere to hide. Doors had been fitted in the doorways, but they were all closed and impossible for her to open.

The voices were only a corridor away. If she didn't get out of sight soon, the approaching Shadows would see her. Maybe they would only be surprised at the sight of her, and they wouldn't try to catch her, but she couldn't take that risk. Desperately, she scanned the corridor again.

Her gaze fell upon a small gap between the edge of the Shadow trap and the corridor wall. It looked barely wide enough, but she could probably squeeze inside. She went in backward as there was no space for her to turn around.

No sooner had she hunkered down and peeked out than a group of people turned the corner and came into view. There were ten or twelve men and women in ordinary office clothes, and they were chatting about everyday stuff. At first, it was impossible to tell who was human and who was a Shadow, but within seconds, the difference was evident.

The humans in the group—about half of them—were puzzled and shocked at the sight of the Shadow trap.

"What the krat's that thing?" one of them asked.

"Is this some kind of joke?" another asked. "I thought we

were going to discuss the building progress, not get taken on a theme park ride."

"Ha," a third said, "that's right. It looks like the entrance to a ghost walk."

"It's just a little diversion before the meeting," one of the Shadows said. "It'll be fun. Come inside."

"Oh, I don't think so," said the person who spoke last. "That place looks scary. I hated those kinds of things when I was a child. I'm going to skip it. I'll wait outside for you folks to finish your fun."

"Me too. I'm not going near it. Look, we appreciate it and all, but I think it might be better if we have the meeting and get it over with. We all have our families to go home to tonight, right?"

The group had reached the trap's entrance. "We insist," said a Shadow. "Come on. It'll only take a minute or two. There's nothing to worry about."

"Really, let's just have the meeting," said a man.

"No," a Shadow replied and pulled out a gun. The other Shadows did the same. The people were in the center, and the aliens surrounded them.

The humans gasped. One of the men tried to grab a weapon. The Shadow holding it shot him at point blank range, destroying his chest. There were screams as his lifeless body crumpled to the floor.

"Inside," commanded a Shadow, all pretense gone. It gestured toward the trap, its face expressionless.

After some hesitation, the humans shuffled in. Some were silently weeping. The Shadows brought up the rear, threatening with their weapons.

A sense of powerlessness and frustration overwhelmed Jas as the group passed inside the trap. The people were going to die and there wasn't anything she could do about it.

If she'd been in her own body, she might have been able to save them, but as a tiny animal, she was powerless. She didn't know what to do.

Go after them, Jas. See what happens.

She jumped a little in surprise. She'd forgotten she was hooked up to the surveillance equipment back at the Lees' home, and that it was recording everything she saw and heard.

It had been Sayen's voice speaking through the linkup in her mind. *You think I should?* she asked mentally. *Maybe I should just find a Shadow we can snatch and get back to you guys.*

No, Sayen replied. *This might be the first and the last chance anyone has of seeing what happens inside a Shadow trap. Haggardy said he couldn't tell what was going on when he was forced inside one with the other officers of the Galathea, do you remember? But you have night vision. You'll be able to see clearly. The better we understand the Shadows, the easier it'll be to defeat them. We're recording all of this, and we can include it in the packet we send to the Transgalactic Council. If we can capture evidence of what the Shadows do to people, we won't need one of our own to show them.*

Okay, I'll see what I can do, Jas replied.

The corridor was empty. She left her hiding place and went through the hexagonal entrance, into the Shadow trap.

She'd first entered a similar structure on K.67092d weeks ago. As she went deeper in, following the sound of people and Shadows ahead, a dull chill settled over her. The feeling was partly due to the frigid atmosphere, and partly due to her memories of taking her fifteen defense units on one Locate, Investigate, Vacate procedure after another of the Shadow traps and failing to find anything wrong. She wished that somehow she could have been more thorough.

If only she'd been able to find something to convince the *Galathea's* master, Loba, of the threat, so many lives could have been saved.

But it was too late for what-might-have-beens. At least now, she finally had her chance to find out what the Shadows did inside their traps.

9

R eplication. Generation. Domination. The plan had to succeed.

Time moved on within the physical realm. The invasion of the planet called Earth was reaching a crisis point.

Most of the schemes had been successful. Their kind now occupied important positions in the controlling and supervising organizations of the planet. They had destroyed and replaced humans in most tiers of the planetary hierarchy. In many cases, replication had taken place without attracting suspicion. In others, humans who had noticed the changes had themselves been quickly targeted and replicated. Soon, replication and generation could occur on a mass scale. The remaining human population would be eradicated.

Until then, it was vital that the galactic powers remain unaware of what was taking place on Earth. A severe threat remained: the six trapped humans.

They had the humans confined within a defended domain. Two were older than the others, and a familial relationship existed between them and one of the younger humans. The group included one adolescent. The two older ones were closely connected with influential agents on Earth and in the galaxy's governing body, named the Transgalactic Council. The other four had been identified upon their arrival. The one who was related to the older ones had infiltrated the digital records that held information on the secret invasion. Despite their best efforts, that human had not been copied and destroyed.

The other three humans were also known. Two had served aboard the starship that had crashed on a trap planet. The sixth human—the adolescent—had escaped from a planet under invasion and come to Earth aboard the same starship. The adolescent had absconded from the center it had been sent to.

Much information was known about these humans. They had inflicted substantial damage and successfully evaded capture many times. The risk their existence posed was extreme, yet all efforts to destroy them had failed. Rather, their menace grew greater. Other humans had been easy to trap and replicate. What made these different?

The threat they posed was growing greater. Already, four of them had broken into a spaceport and stolen a critical item. It was only after investigation had established *what* was stolen that its significance was realized. The air attack to destroy the humans and the purloined machine had failed. Now, they would be able to use the device to identify a human replicant.

The event increased the risk of defeat. Replication and generation depended on the replicants' ability to blend into the local population. If the humans used the machine to root out replicants, the effects would be disastrous. Even worse, if the humans alerted the galactic powers of the invasion, all their plans would fail. Past experience of failure told them what would happen then. Wholesale slaughter. A massacre of their kind. No opportunity to return to the void. No chance of life within the physical realm or the ethereal place that was their home.

All resources were to be devoted to eliminating these humans. Already, devices newly acquired had been used to shut down external communication to galactic and intra-planetary receivers. Now, all new weapons obtained were to be targeted at the trapped humans. It was vital that they were eradicated.

To add to the difficulties, as well as the persistent threat of the six renegade humans, an old enemy had emerged within the void. A never-ending battle had resumed. Beings who chose to thwart their attempts to infiltrate the physical realm had discovered their schemes and, once again, risen up against them.

Through an infinity of nothingness, the two sides tussled. Never tiring and unable to die, the fighters fought without respite, whirling in patterns of ether and light, fleeing only to be recaptured, and securing their opponents only to have to eventually release them.

Two escapes were open: Earth and other planets of the galaxy, where they could live on within replicants, or a final defeat of their enemy within the void. If they could achieve both, victory would be sweet. They could live on forever within their corporeal and ethereal forms. They could enjoy physical pleasures and the freedom of the void, and move between the realms without restraint.

They had only to destroy the trapped humans and vanquish their ancient foe. Then, eternity and infinite space could be theirs.

10

Carl passed a hand over his eyes. Jas stopped the playback of what she'd witnessed inside the Shadow trap. They were alone in the basement of the Lees' home. Sayen had refused to watch the replay of the vid. Seeing the events through the spy fox's eyes as it had happened was plenty, she'd said, before going upstairs to talk to her parents. Carl was wishing he'd followed her lead.

Though the recording had been a confusion of figures and movement, he had seen enough detail to understand the terrible events. He didn't think he would ever be able to forget the images of the men and women sinking—*dissolving* —into the floor, or erase from his memory their cries of terror and agony.

Jas had been able to view the scene first hand because she'd watched it through the surveillance device's visual sensors. She'd estimated that if she'd been watching with human eyes, she wouldn't have seen a thing in the darkness. The Shadows had retreated to another chamber, and the dim beams from their distant flashlights were the only illumination. The victims had acted as though they were blind.

"Krat," Carl said. "I never even imagined what they went through. Margret, the officers on the *Galathea*, the governor on Dawn, and the soldiers...Jas, do you think *that's* what happened to my parents?"

Jas reached out and took his hand. "I said I didn't think you should watch. If you hadn't insisted on seeing what the Shadows did, I wouldn't have shown you. It's probably best not to think about it."

He placed his other hand over hers. "I get that you wanted to protect me, but I suppose it's better that I know. We've got to *destroy* these misborns, Jas. We've got to take them out—forever."

"I know. And we will. We will. But wait a moment. Watch the next part."

She restarted the vid. The human victims had entirely disappeared, absorbed by the Shadow trap floor, but the Shadows returned and stood as if waiting for something. They pointed their flashlights at one wall of the chamber.

After a short time, a bulge appeared in the wall. A lump of dark gray material protruded. A little farther down the wall, a similar bulge appeared.

"Look," Jas said, pointing at the first gray lump.

Carl leaned forward to peer at the screen more closely. The surface was changing, melting like ice cream on a sunny day. The material shifted around, and lines and irregular shapes appeared. "It's a face," he exclaimed. "So, this is...?"

Jas nodded. "This is how the victims' Shadows emerge. Watch."

When the lump had changed into a recognizably human, dark gray head, it began to struggle, as if it were trying to fight its way out of the wall. A smaller lump appeared below the head, and another below that. The struggling head moved forward, dragging out a torso behind it. As the body appeared, it grew more defined. It moved out into the room, pulling its legs and arms free, until finally a human form stood unsteadily in the chamber.

While this was going on, more human-like figures were pushing through the wall and struggling free. Soon, a group of new Shadows were standing together, the same number as the victims who had been murdered. The aliens were breathing, taking on color, and moving about uncertainly. The original Shadows went forward to help them. It was like witnessing a set of bizarre, horrifying births.

After some time, when the new Shadows had gotten used to their bodies, all of them left the chamber. Jas turned off the recording.

Carl exhaled as tension left him. "What did you do then?" he asked.

"I had to follow them—at a distance," Jas replied. "Even the visual sensors Sayen's dad installed in the fox needed *some* light to operate, and it was pitch black in there. Without light, I would never have found my way out of the place. As well as the darkness, it's a maze. I remember the same from the LIVs I conducted when we were aboard the *Galathea*. I needed my helmet's navigation function to find my way out again. I guess that's part of the trap. If you wander in, or you're tempted or forced inside, I don't know how anyone would ever find their way out. I don't know how Haggardy did it."

"Do you still think he's a Shadow?"

"I don't know. Maybe he is, or maybe he's just the same misborn he's always been. It doesn't matter anymore. There were Shadows here on Earth before we returned. One more or less isn't going to make a difference. But, Carl, we don't know for sure if that's what's happened to your parents. No Shadows of them were waiting for you when you got home."

"That's right. I wouldn't have stood a chance against two Shadows catching me by surprise."

"I wonder what did happen to them."

Carl smiled ruefully. "Knowing my folks, they wouldn't have let themselves become victims of the Shadows. They'd rather have died."

The significance of his words hit him, and he reached out to Jas and drew her close, burying his face in the crook of her neck. She wrapped her arms around him. They stayed that way for a while, until his emotions were spent.

Carl was exhausted. The last time he'd slept had been on the mountainside where Ozment had taken them. It seemed an age ago, and there would be no opportunity for rest that night. The bombardment from the Shadows was continuing, a dazzling display of power. They could break through at any moment. He and Makey had to take out the suppressor as soon as possible.

After that, who knew what would happen? It seemed likely that Carl's next sleep would be his last, but now that he'd finally accepted that his parents were gone, maybe that didn't matter so much anymore.

On the far side of the basement, the elevator chimed, and the doors opened. Sayen stepped out. "Have you two finished watching that vid yet? I came to tell you that the Shadow attack has stopped for the moment. The skies are clear."

"Yeah, all done," Jas replied. She turned off the screen.

"What do you think?" Sayen asked as she walked over. "Enough evidence to show the Council? Or do we need a real live Shadow too?"

"I guess the Council might be persuaded the vid's been

faked," Jas replied, "but it's enough to raise their suspicions, especially if your parents send it. Even so, I still think we should catch a Shadow and send them the positive result from the scanner. No one could argue with that, and it gives us something to do until the truck's ready."

"Great," Sayen said. "I was getting bored just sitting around. Ha, it's weird. I would never have wanted to do anything like this before. Now I can't wait. I wish my brother were here. He always used to tease me for being a little mouse. I think he'd be proud of me."

"We're all proud of you," Jas said.

"That's right," Carl said. "How are your parents doing with their alterations to the truck?"

"About another hour they said. You should see Makey. He's in heaven. I don't think I've ever seen him happier."

"Do we have enough time for a short expedition?" Jas asked.

"Yeah, I think so. I'll ask Daddy if he can turn off the defenses for a moment so we can go through the secret gate and arrange a time for him to turn them off again so we can get in. What do you think?"

"Sounds good" Jas said. "I didn't tell you," she said to Carl. "After I came out of the trap, I found one of the Shadows asleep alone in a room. It shouldn't take more than fifteen to twenty minutes to slip out, grab her, and slip back in again."

"It's a woman?" Carl asked.

"No, it's that little girl you wanted me to grab when we arrived. For some reason, she's sleeping apart from the adults. The others seem to be sticking in groups."

11

———

Sayen waited as Jas checked the time. They were in a wooded section of the estate, but near the house this time, at the secret gate.

"Thirty seconds," Jas said.

They were wearing dark clothes, and Sayen's father had given them something to wear over their heads that covered their faces and necks. The material allowed them to breathe easily, but prevented light from reflecting off their faces and revealing them in the darkness. Both also carried two weapons strapped to their hips in case something went wrong and they had to protect themselves. Sayen was bringing a sedative to inject into the sleeping Shadow so that she wouldn't wake up and raise the alarm.

"Fifteen seconds," said Jas.

Sayen got ready to open the secret gate. Her father had pointed out the barely visible outline of it in the fence. Beyond that point, all was dark. The sky had clouded over and the moon and stars weren't visible. Sayen blinked and used her night vision. She saw no forms other than the sparse desert plants. There was no sign of any movement.

They had to get the timing right. Touching the gate at the wrong moment would mean certain death. They had only five seconds to go through and close it behind them. They couldn't risk turning off the defenses for longer. The aerial attack could recommence at any time. Once they were through, they had twenty minutes to find and bring back the Shadow. If they missed the time scheduled for their return, they would be locked out.

"Five, four, three, two—" Jas said.

Sayen reached out.

"One."

She opened the gate. They stepped through, and she pulled it closed.

"Let's go," Jas said.

"Wait," said Sayen. The gate had disappeared into the fence. Once they left it, they would have a hard time finding it again. "Get some rocks," she said to Jas.

"I see what you mean. Good idea."

She waited while Jas gathered a few rocks. After stacking them in a small pile in front of the gate, they set off to catch their Shadow.

Sayen was glad she had something to do while they waited for her parents to prepare the truck for its assault on the Shadow's suppressor. She knew she should really have gone to check on Erielle—the woman was unwell and alone in a strange house—but she couldn't bring herself to. Not after their argument. She didn't know what to make of what they'd both said. Her mother had told her that Erielle was spending most of the time asleep anyway.

The truth was, though she didn't agree with the underworlder, she could see why she thought as she did. Though the arguments Sayen had used to defend her parents were all true, and she loved them deeply, she wasn't sure she could excuse their lifestyle now that she'd heard Erielle's opinion, not even to herself. Why were they so highly paid? Did they really deserve everything they had? What had they meant when they said they helped the work against 'enemies of the Government'? How were the devices they made used? Were they used for good? Could her parents even tell?

On the other hand, Sayen was sure that all the money in the world couldn't fix what was wrong with their society, nor improve the lives of the worst off, like the underworlders, over the long term. So, in a way, both she and Erielle were right. She just didn't think she would ever get the woman to see it that way. The underworlder was passionate about the inequalities and injustices she saw.

It seemed inevitable that they would have to part ways. There could be no future for two people with such different backgrounds and who held such different views. Sayen just didn't feel ready to have that conversation with Erielle yet.

They were nearing the road. "Crossing that is going to be the toughest part," said Jas. "Lights from the Shadows' building reveal everything for quite a distance. We'll have to go far out of our way to cross in darkness. That's why I told your father we needed twenty minutes."

"Okay," Sayen replied, though it seemed they would be cutting it very fine. She supposed Jas knew what she was doing.

They moved through the desert until the light from the Shadow's building was faint, then crossed over the road in little more than a heartbeat. Even with her enhanced hearing, Sayen detected no sounds coming from the aliens' building. They began their approach.

In another few minutes, they were squatting below an open window. According to what Jas had seen, the Shadow girl was asleep in this room, alone. The plan was that Sayen would go inside, sedate the sleeping girl, then lift her and pass her out to Jas. When Sayen was outside again, they would take the Shadow back to the estate.

She stood to peer over the windowsill. Inside, all was dark. She heard breathing. Using her night vision, all she could see was bare floor and walls.

Jas touched her leg. When she looked down, the hunkered-down woman spread her hands wide in a questioning gesture. Sayen raised flat palm. *Wait.* She listened again. Someone was definitely in the room. No. She could hear two people breathing. She lifted two fingers to Jas, who grimaced in response.

Sayen frowned as she listened again. There were definitely two sets of breathing sounds. One was soft and light. That could be the Shadow girl. The other, though, was even softer, lighter, and faster. If Sayen had been forced to guess, she would have said there was a baby in the room. Had the Shadows taken a baby? The thought sent a shudder down her spine.

Jas pointed at her timer. Sayen had to act now or it would be too late.

She grabbed the windowsill and pulled herself up and over in one smooth motion. She checked her momentum as she landed right next to the Shadow, who was sleeping under the window. The girl's eyes opened at the sound of Sayen's arrival. Her mouth also opened to shout or scream. Sayen quickly pressed down on the child's face with one hand, muffling her voice, and with the other hand, she delivered the sedative into her bare neck.

As the girl's eyes closed and her body went limp, Sayen glanced around. Where was the second breather she'd heard? The room was empty. The girl was alone as she'd been when Jas had last seen her. There was no time to figure out the mystery. She had to pass the Shadow out of the window, and they had to get back home in time for the momentary defense shutdown.

The Shadow girl was lying on a pile of clothes and blankets beneath an adult woman's coat. Sayen reached under the coat to grab her around her waist and pull her out. As she did so, her hand encountered something soft, warm, and furry. She pulled back in surprise and lifted the coat to see what it was. A cat was curled up next to the girl. After Sayen exposed it, the animal took fright. It jumped onto the girl and out of the window. It must have landed on the waiting Jas, because Sayen heard her gasp from outside.

The Shadow had been cuddling a cat. Or had the cat only approached her for warmth and she'd let it stay? There was no time to figure it out.

Sayen lifted the girl's limp body and lowered her into Jas's waiting arms. She vaulted out the window and down onto the desert sand. Jas was already running, carrying the Shadow child. Sayen quickly caught up to her.

"Pass her to me," she said to Jas. "I won't feel her weight at all."

Jas handed over the Shadow, and Sayen put her over her shoulder.

The aliens in the building didn't seem to notice the missing girl, because no sight or sound of pursuit came from behind. They ran from the revealing lights and into the darkness, to the point where they could cross the road unseen.

As they approached her home, Sayen saw movement at the front. The truck was pulling around from the back onto the driveway, with Makey at the wheel. Her parents must have finished the modifications. They were nearly ready to destroy the suppressor.

She and Jas had their Shadow. With the information they would be able to send, the Transgalactic Council couldn't ignore the Shadow invasion. They had to dispatch the Unity forces to drive them out. Earth would be saved, even if she, her parents, and her friends might not live to see it.

12

───────

"**Y**ou all right, mate?" Carl called down to Makey from his position behind the weapon on the roof of the truck. They had less than two minutes before Sayen's dad would drop the force field and they would set out on their mission.

"Yeah, I'm fine," the kid replied. "All set. And you?"

"I'm all set, too."

"We have time to swap places if you want. You know I'm a better shot than you."

Carl laughed. He liked the kid's spark. "In your dreams. I was shooting rumpabugs before you were born. Now shut up and concentrate on driving this thing straight. Have you got the shields up?"

"'Course."

"Then let's wait for the signal."

Carl settled himself back in his seat, his palms resting on the controls of the weapon Sayen's mother had modified. Above him was the shield Mr. Lee had constructed. It was a smooth rotating dome, open only a slit where the barrel of the weapon ended. He wasn't totally blind to what was happening outside, however: a visual of the sky was provided by an interface screen between his controls.

He hardly recognized the weapon as Ozment's out-of-date missile launcher. His brief instructions from Mrs. Lee had been basically to tell him to let the weapon do its thing —that its capabilities far exceeded human powers. His presence was only required in case the automatic targeting got taken out by a hit. Then, it would operate manually, but only to the extent of Carl's ability.

In case he lost targeting *and* visual on the interface, Mr. Lee had fitted an explosive eject system for the dome. It was a desperate measure, but Carl would be able to continue firing by sight. He hoped his skills would be sufficient to protect the truck until Makey had done his job. If they survived *and* made it back, that would be a bonus.

The truck began to vibrate. Makey had started the engine and was driving. It was time.

As the truck started toward the gate, Carl flipped the switch to activate the weapon. The display lit up, and the barrel swiveled right, taking Carl in his seat with it. On the screen, a large heli was revealed. The Shadows had seen the truck begin to move and had launched their response. Concentric lines moved down the screen to the heli's center. The weapon had identified its first target before they were even outside the gates.

The screen flashed repeatedly, as if the weapon were begging Carl to fire. He had to wait. If he fired, the charge wouldn't penetrate the force field.

"Nearly there," Makey called, aware of the fact that Carl could see nothing but sky.

He heard a rumble as the estate gates opened.

MAKEY HAD ARGUED SO hard to be allowed to do this, and tried so hard to get the adults to stop treating him like a kid. Yet when it came to it, he still felt like a kid inside. Maybe he'd been wrong to push so hard. Now, everyone was relying on him, and he wasn't sure he was up to it. Maybe he should have let someone else drive the truck.

His palms were sweaty on the steering wheel. Through the slit in the cab's shields, he could see Mr. Lee standing at his front door, holding a small control device. He held one hand up in the air, its fingers spread. Five. Five seconds until Makey had to begin the drive down to the gate.

It was too late to back out now.

He gripped the steering wheel hard. He could do it. He *would* do it. He wouldn't let everyone down.

One finger on Mr. Lee's hand dropped. Four. Another finger. Three. Two. One.

Makey pressed the gas, and the truck approached the gates. He was counting in his head. He had ten seconds until Mr. Lee would open the gates and drop the force field long enough for him to drive through.

He had one job. Get to the correct side of the building and drive right into it as fast as he could. It was vital that he destroy the suppressor. Otherwise everyone's effort would be wasted. No message would get through to the Trans-galactic Council, and Earth would fall to the Shadows.

His stomach clenched. It was all on him. Everything they'd done up to that point, everything that everyone had gone through, was so that he—a kid—could do this.

"Nearly there," he called to Carl.

Almost as he was upon them, the gates parted. In another moment, he was through. Immediately, the truck rocked with the force of an explosion on the roof, and another explosion to the right caused it to buck violently.

Makey wrenched the steering wheel to bring the swerving vehicle back under his control. He was veering too far to the left. Now he was too far to the right. He couldn't seem to keep it straight. The truck was heading off the road and into the desert on either side, almost out of control.

Flames erupted to his right as a heli hit the ground. Carl had got one. The truck shuddered again as they took another direct hit. On the left was another that sent deep vibrations through the cab and into his bones and teeth.

Something was wrong. The truck wasn't driving like it should. It was leaning and juddering hard. The Shadows had succeeded in shooting out tires on one side. Carl had told him this might happen, but he'd said the truck would still go, only it would be harder to control her.

Makey brought the vehicle around. The building appeared in his sight. He only had to keep the truck straight and get her to top speed before impact. If he could only do that, it would be enough.

THEY WERE BARELY through the gates before Carl fired the weapon. The heli that the gun held in its sights exploded and toppled from the sky, but before it hit the ground, the weapon was already swiveling around to another target. Carl fired again and caught a glimpse of a missile just before it dissolved in midair. *Missiles?* The Shadows weren't only attacking from the air, they were firing at them from a base far away from the estate. *Krat.* He had no chance of finding and destroying the base using the weapon in the truck. They were vulnerable to every missile launched at them, and so was Sayen's parents' estate.

He had no time to think about that. The weapon was

swiveling rapidly once more. A shuttle was passing overhead, and both its guns were firing. Streaks of fire streamed down toward the truck, but on their way an answering bolt crossed them, traveling in the opposite direction into the heart of the shuttle's engine. The space vehicle split apart like a massive exploding firework. Flaming debris was scattered across the sky.

The truck took another hit from the missile launcher. It nearly turned the vehicle on its side. Carl was amazed at Makey's skills at reacting to the deluge of hits, keeping the truck going. He guessed that they were driving toward the building.

With a deafening crack, the dome above him blew away. A hit had triggered the eject device. The cold desert wind chilled his skin, and he saw the predawn sky with its clearing clouds and fading stars. The sky held more than stars, however. Carl was being carried around in his seat again as the automatic targeting system locked onto another aircraft.

The gun roared, and Carl's seat kicked back as it fired. The weapon was better than any he'd ever known, but would it be enough? The top of the building rose up at the edge of his vision. They were nearly there. They'd nearly made it. A stream of fire ran across the truck's roof, searing the weapon. Flames flickered from Carl's clothes, and for several seconds he battled to prevent the fire from enveloping him, scorching his hands as he extinguished the flames.

As his panic eased, he became aware that he and the weapon were no longer moving. The hit had taken out the automatic targeting. If he were to defend the truck and Makey, it was now entirely down to him. He grabbed the controls and spun the weapon around, searching the skies for a target.

A massive boom sounded to his right, and the truck began to topple. It leaned so far, Carl knew it would never recover. The power of the blast and the speed of their falling meant Makey would never right the vehicle. They hadn't reached the Shadows' building or the suppressor inside. It was over. As Carl was thrown to the side in the falling truck, more of the building became visible. They were only a few tens of meters from it. They'd almost made it. Almost.

A heli appeared overhead. Was this the aircraft that had defeated them? Had the Shadow pilot come to gloat over his victory? With an enormous effort, Carl wrenched the weapon around and fired a final shot as the truck hit the rocky desert floor. He was thrown from the vehicle. Momentum carried both he and the truck forward. Carl tumbled along the dry dirt; the truck slid along on its side with a dreadful screeching and showers of sparks.

As Carl finished rolling, he leapt to his feet to run after the vehicle. He had to reach Makey and get him out of the cab before Shadows emerged from the building. They might have failed to destroy the suppressor, but that didn't mean they would give up. They would fight to the last.

The sound of roaring came from overhead, and the ground lit up with reflected light. Carl looked up to see that the heli he'd fired at—the one that had delivered the decisive blow—was falling from the sky.

With his last effort, he'd hit it. Carl smiled in grim satisfaction, but his expression turned to one of joyous disbelief as he realized the trajectory of the doomed vehicle. It was heading straight for the Shadow building. It was going to hit it on the corner they'd been aiming at.

The truck finally slid to a halt only meters from the building. Carl sped up. The heli hit and crashed through the brick wall. As shattered fragments of brick sprayed out, the inferno that had once been the heli exploded.

Carl was at the truck's cab. The heat from the downed heli was almost unbearable. The cab's shields were still up. He peered through the slit and just made out an unconscious Makey inside. He had only seconds before the metal of the shields heated up and fried the kid. But how could he get to him? He tugged at the door handles, burning his hands. They were jammed. He hammered on the steel shields, but Makey didn't stir.

Despair gnawed at Carl. He couldn't let the kid die. He screamed at him through the window slit, and as he did, he saw the dark hole of the tunnel entrance behind the seats. Of course. In a moment, he was at the roof of the truck where it lay on the ground. He grabbed the edge of the tunnel and pulled himself up. Feet first, he climbed down into the chokingly hot cab.

Makey was out cold from a blow to the head. Carl undid his seat belt. Somehow, he managed to maneuver the kid out of his seat and pull him up through the tunnel. He gulped the cool desert air as he emerged onto the roof with the unconscious young man and tumbled with him to the ground.

Movement caught his eye. He looked up. They were surrounded by Shadows.

13

———

Jas and Sayen had made it back to the fence surrounding the Lees' estate just in time. They carried the unconscious Shadow child inside and to the elevator to take her down to the basement. The Lee Family androids had put the scanner there after removing it from the back of the truck. The Shadow girl was about ten years old—the human victim had been about ten, Jas corrected herself.

Like all the aliens, the Shadow was indistinguishable from the child whose place she had taken. Her hair was shoulder length and loose, and long bangs hung down as her head lolled. She had freckles across her nose, and two of her front teeth were missing.

"Where was the cat when you went into the room?" Jas asked Sayen as they neared the scanner. The androids had connected it to a power supply. It was a simple, flat-bottomed tube on a waist-high base. Jas noted it was similar to the one she'd been scanned in when she'd first arrived on Dawn. An interface at one end displayed one word: Ready.

"It was sleeping with her. They were both under a coat. I

frightened it, I think, when I lifted the coat. That was why it took off."

"It was cuddled up with her? She was cuddling a cat?"

"That was how it looked. It could've crept in there by itself after she was asleep, I guess."

"It must have, don't you think?" Jas asked. "Kinda weird if it didn't. I mean, I never thought of the Shadows liking other creatures. They don't even seem to like each other that much."

"It's hard to tell what they like or dislike. They're aliens. They might not even have likes and dislikes. But I agree, it does seem weird. I don't think I've ever been more surprised in my life than when I took that coat off of her and found a cat there. I was expecting a baby or something."

Jas tried not to contemplate the idea of a baby experiencing what she'd seen happen to the humans in the Shadow trap.

"Come on," Sayen went on. "Let's do this. My parents said they have the packet ready to send the minute the guys destroy the suppressor. We just need to upload the readings from the scanner."

They laid the girl out on the belt. Sayen touched the interface, and it started up, moving the Shadow into the tube. Soon, they were looking at the soles of her bare, dirty feet. The scanner hummed quietly.

To her surprise, Jas found she was holding her breath. She had this sudden, irrational hope that the child wasn't a Shadow, even though it would mean that their plans to alert the Transgalactic Council might fail. She didn't want to think about the victim's death, or the Shadow's strange affection for an Earth animal. She couldn't reconcile her understanding of the aliens with the image of this little girl sleeping with her arms wrapped around a cat.

"Look," Sayen said. She was gazing at the interface screen.

Jas joined her at the display. It showed a 3D graphic of the child's body, split into sections. A faint glow emanated from all parts of the girl. As Jas watched it, the graphic disappeared and was replaced by the words, Shadow Confirmed.

Her heart sank.

Sayen was already swiping the screen, capturing the results and sending them onward to the message packet her parents had prepared.

"We did it, Jas," she said as she touched the icon to close the display. "After all this time, we finally did it."

"Yeah," Jas replied half-heartedly.

"What's wrong?"

"I don't know. I guess I can't quite believe that she's a Shadow." Jas sighed. "So, what now? When will the sedative wear off? And what do we do with her then?" She realized she hadn't thought about what they would do with the captured alien.

"She should start coming around in another ten minutes or so. Then—"

Behind them, the elevator pinged. They turned to see Mrs. Lee step out. "We got the results, honey. And Daddy's sending the packet now to the nearest deep space link. When the Council receives it, it shouldn't take them more than a few days to get to Earth and begin investigating."

"He's sending the packet?" Jas asked. "You mean you have deep space comm? Carl and Makey destroyed the suppressor?"

"Yes, just a few moments ago. The waves blinked out to nothing."

"But what about the guys?" asked Jas. "Are they back?"

"Not yet. The truck turned over before it hit the building. But one of the helis Carl downed smashed into it instead. That must have been what destroyed the suppressor."

Sayen and Jas shared a look. "Let's go," Sayen said.

"You're going out there?" said Mrs. Lee. "Oh, Sayen, do you have to?"

They were already running for the elevator. "Yes, Mama, I do. They're my friends."

IT TOOK Sayen several minutes to persuade her father to turn off the force field so they could go out to rescue Carl and Makey. He repeated that he would go himself rather than let her risk her life. But she pointed out that he had to stay home. He couldn't leave her mother and their sick guest, Erielle, alone.

"Be careful out there," were his final words as he turned off the force field. He had a look on his face like he thought he would never see his daughter again.

Jas had armed them both with extra blasters before leaving the house. She held one in each hand as, together, they ran across the road toward the burning building. No time for precautionary measures now. If Carl and Makey were still alive, every second would count in keeping them that way.

The Shadows' building was rapidly turning into an inferno. Flames rose twice as high as the walls, and a dull roaring filled the air. They were still far away when Jas felt the heat of the fire on her face.

The sun was rising, but the light from the fire was brighter. Jas could only just make out the end of the truck. It was also on fire, and the dark shapes of men and women were outlined in the light. She could vaguely see some kind of struggle going on.

"Krat. Sayen, the Shadows have them."

"You tackle them from this side," Sayen said. "I'm going around the back."

"But—"

Sayen was already leaving, running at her impossibly fast speed toward the rear of the building.

At the fight with the Shadows, someone was lifting a large rock as if they were getting ready to bring it down heavily on an opponent's head.

Raising her weapon and aiming as she ran, Jas fired. She got the Shadow holding the rock in the back. It looked down, incredulous, at the smoking hole that appeared in its chest before dropping limply to the ground. The rest of them turned. She fired again, and another Shadow fell.

They were armed. As one raised its weapon to return fire, Carl plowed into its side, sending it flying into some of the others. Makey was sitting on the sand, looking barely conscious.

More Shadows raised their weapons. There were too many of them. Jas could never shoot them all, and Carl had been disarmed.

Just as Jas was accepting this was her last fight, a cry of rage rose above the crackle of the flames. The cry had come from the burning truck. The Shadows turned toward the sound in puzzlement.

Sayen was on top of the vehicle, standing within the blaze. She leapt down. She was firing, and she was on fire. Shadows fell at each blast of her weapon, and Jas shot down more of them. They only stopped firing when the rest of the aliens fled.

Suddenly, Carl had Sayen on the ground. He was rolling her in the dirt, putting out the flames. Her clothes were little more than blackened shreds.

Makey staggered to his feet, shaking his head.

"You did it," Jas exclaimed to Carl. "The suppressor's destroyed. Sayen's parents have sent the packet."

"*We* did it," Carl said. "We all did."

The Shadows seemed to have retreated. Sayen and Carl were burned, and Makey had taken a severe blow to the head, but they'd survived. Carl and Jas hugged. They held the kid's arms to support him, and all four of them turned toward Sayen's home.

It was at that moment that the mansion took a direct hit.

14

—————

"Krat," Sayen exclaimed. One side of the front of the beautiful house was ruined, and smoke was already pouring from the windows nearby. The next second, she was gone. She was running toward her home, her raggedy clothes trailing behind her.

Jas, Carl, and especially Makey, struggled to keep up with their friend.

"What's firing at the house?" Jas asked Carl, scanning the early morning sky. "I thought you shot everything down?"

"They've got a missile launcher somewhere out in the desert," he replied. "It almost destroyed the truck too. The automatic targeting was taking out the missiles, but it couldn't zero in on the launcher."

Another missile screamed overhead, and as they watched, it tore through the electrified fence. The house took another hit.

"Look at that," Carl said, looking behind. The Shadows had reappeared and were running toward the estate. "Do you think they're after us or Sayen's parents?"

"I don't know," Jas replied. "Whatever it is they want to do, it isn't going to be good. We have to catch up to Sayen. She can't take them all on by herself."

But it wasn't easy to catch up. Makey could barely run. Carl and Jas were partly supporting him and partly dragging him along.

Sayen had reached the gate. She leapt over its ruins and went speeding up the driveway. The other three struggled after her. Jas saw her swing open the front door and disappear inside.

By the time the other three reached the same spot, Makey was nearly unconscious again. He collapsed onto the front steps.

"Take him upstairs, Carl," Jas said, glancing over her shoulder. The remaining Shadows were clambering over the ruins of the gate. "Take him to Erielle's room, so I know where you all are. I'm going to find Sayen and her parents. We might escape the Shadows yet."

Carl put his hands under Makey's arms and hauled the kid to his feet. Like a drunken couple, the two made their way up the staircase. Jas followed, helping to support the unconscious Makey. At the top, they parted ways.

Carl said. "After I get him to Erielle's room, I'm going to give Erielle a gun and lock them in together. Then I'm going to come and find you. Take care, Jas."

"I will," she replied and gave him a fleeting smile.

As she ran to Mr. Lee's room, another explosion rocked the house. She grabbed a desk to steady herself. It would only be a matter of minutes before the place was rubble. The elevator was at the basement. She called it and, too slowly, it rose.

As the doors opened, Jas's heart missed a beat. The interior was splattered with blood. Whose blood, she didn't dare to think. She stepped inside. As the elevator went down, she readied her weapon. Whatever was waiting for her at the bottom would see the elevator was descending. She pressed her back against the corner to the right and aimed the muzzle of her gun at the crack between the doors. She aimed low.

The elevator chimed. Before the doors had opened more than a slit, Jas fired. A laser beam returned her fire, scoring a deep burn in the wall opposite the door. The doors opened wide. No more laser beams were discharged. Jas peeked out. She'd hit the Shadow girl. She was on the floor, and Sayen and her parents were behind her. Mr. Lee's head was streaming with blood.

"Thanks, Jas," Sayen said as she saw her. "The Shadow was about to kill me. Daddy had forced her down back here when she tried to escape, but she'd gotten the upper hand."

"No problem," Jas replied. "But hurry. We have to get out. There are Shadows in the house. We have to collect Erielle, Makey, and Carl, and leave. Now."

At the end of her sentence, the lights flickered and went out. The basement was suddenly pitch black.

"The power supply's been hit," Mrs. Lee exclaimed.

"Oh no," came Sayen's voice in the darkness. "How are we going to get out? The elevator won't operate without power."

"It's okay," said Mr. Lee. "There are stairs for just such an emergency. We only have to get to them. Everybody, join hands. Follow me."

"Be careful," Jas said. "The Shadow girl will be coming around soon."

"What? You didn't kill her?" asked Sayen.

"No. I didn't know who I might be shooting at. It could have been one of you three. I set my weapon to stun."

"Krat," Sayen said.

"Sayen, that isn't very polite," said Mrs. Lee.

Sayen sighed. "Sorry, Mama."

They went farther across the workroom, Mr. Lee slowly guiding them around the workbenches and machinery. After a short while, he bumped into something. "Ah. I believe we're nearly at the wall. Yes, here it is. Now we just follow it to the left. If we're lucky, I should be able to locate the door handle."

"Hey," said a voice in the distance. A little girl's voice. "Where are you? Where are y'all going?"

Jas's stomach clenched. The Shadow sounded exactly like a sad, lost child.

"Don't answer," whispered Sayen.

"I heard you," said the girl. "I know where you are. I'm coming over. Wait for me."

Jas could see nothing but darkness. She could feel nothing but Sayen's hand and the smooth wall they were following.

"Are you here?" asked the Shadow. Already, it sounded like she was nearby. "Please answer. I want to find you. I have to find you. I have to get out. Please take me with you. Don't leave me down here all alone."

A quiet expression of satisfaction came from in front. Mr. Lee had found the entrance to the staircase.

"I can hear you," said the girl. "Wait for me. I'm coming."

There was a rustle and a creak as Mr. Lee opened the door. Jas felt Sayen's tug, signaling her to follow. She felt the door's edge. Sayen let go of her as she went through.

A soft, small child's hand plucked at Jas's arm. She froze.

"There you are," said the Shadow, excitement in her voice.

Horror and dread overcame Jas. She kicked out. Her foot

met its mark and sank into something soft and warm before sending the thing flying. There was a shriek. Jas bolted through the door and slammed it closed. She was in the stairwell, but she was still in darkness.

"Here, Jas," called Sayen. Following the sound of her friend's voice, she tripped over a step. Scrabbling sounded from the other side of the door. The Shadow was trying to find the door handle. Jas hadn't been able to lock it. The girl would be through the door and after them at any moment.

She raced upstairs. Somewhere above, light appeared, casting a faint illumination down the steps. Mr. Lee had reached the top and opened the door into an upper level room with a window.

From below came the sound of creaking as the door opened followed by light footsteps running up. Jas broke into a cold sweat. She felt a special horror about the cat-loving Shadow girl. Something about her was especially fearful, and yet Jas wasn't sure she could kill her.

Jas emerged into the room at the top of the stairs. She slammed the door shut. "That *thing's* coming up after us," she panted.

"Don't worry, sugar," Mrs. Lee said. "Not a problem." She jammed a chair under the doorknob.

"Which way to Erielle's room?" Jas asked.

"Follow me," Sayen replied.

"Have you noticed something?" Mr Lee asked as they left the bedroom. "The bombardment has stopped."

"Probably because Shadows are in the building," Jas said. "They don't want to kill their own kind. They must be planning to capture us, or pick us off one by one."

15

"Erielle," Sayen called through the door. She didn't want to take the woman by surprise. If she was armed, opening the door without announcing herself could be disastrous.

"Thank krat," came Erielle's reply. "Get in here."

Sayen went inside to find Erielle in bed with Makey lying unconscious next to her. Carl was sitting down with his arms folded. The two android servants were standing over him as if on guard duty.

"What's going on?" Jas asked.

"They wouldn't let me leave," Carl replied in an exasperated tone.

"Sir, Ma'am," said the female android, Florence. "It appears that the estate is under attack. We took the initiative to keep our guests safe while we awaited your further instructions."

"And you did a wonderful job," Sayen's mother replied. "Now I have another job for you. First—Jas, Carl, please give our servants a weapon."

Jas held her blaster protectively to her chest. "What?

Why?"

"Because they're going to defend us. I've reprogrammed them with military skills, as far as I was able. Their primary function now is to save our lives. That's why they wouldn't let Carl leave the room."

"Oh, I see." Jas handed over a gun.

Mrs. Lee addressed the androids. "Now, I want you both to understand that the creatures that are roaming this house and looking for us are not human. They may look, sound, and act human, but they are not. Do you understand that? Do you believe me?"

"Yes, we do, Ma'am," chorused the two androids.

"That means you are not breaking any fundamental law by shooting at them, right?" she continued. "In fact, you would be doing us an enormous favor. Do you think you'll be able to do that? If you kill the invaders, it would help us. It would give us a chance to escape."

"We can do that, Ma'am."

"Wonderful," said Sayen's father, looking out the window. "I think it's high time we got the krat out of here."

"Craven," exclaimed Sayen's mother.

Erielle pushed down her covers and pulled herself out of bed and onto her crutches. She refused all offers of help. Sayen picked up Makey, and they went out into the corridor.

"Where now?" Jas asked.

"To the helis on the roof," Mrs. Lee said. "We'll never get out with Shadows all over the house looking for us. Now that the force field's down, we might as well take our chances in the sky. Was that your plan, Craven?"

"Exactly, my dear," her husband replied.

The android servants went one way to head off the Shadows, and the humans went the other. Sayen's father led them away from the main staircase and into the smaller corridors. A Shadow wandered into view, and Carl shot it. Sayen hoped the alien died before it had a chance to tell the others where they were.

She knew this part of the house well. She'd often played hide and seek with her brother there when they were children. It was also the quickest route to the roof. She'd walked it during her short-lived stint at the Global Government Security Headquarters.

Wisps of smoke were following them down the corridor, and the air was filled with the smell of burning. They would have to leave soon if they didn't want to go up in flames with the rest of the place. Sayen's heart sank at the knowledge that the only home she'd ever known would soon be gone. But they'd sent the packet to the Transgalactic Council, and with a little luck, they could escape the Shadows pursuing them and find some place to hide out while waiting for the Council to come to Earth's aid.

A cry echoed out. Someone had been shot not far away. The androids had their backs. She hoped they would last out a while longer.

They redoubled their pace. Soon, they were running. Poor Erielle was hobbling along as fast as she could on her crutches.

"Here we are at last," Sayen's father said. He opened the door to the stairway that led to the roof. The corridor echoed with footsteps. Sayen turned to see several Shadows running toward them. They'd broken through the androids' defenses. Jas fired, killing the leader, but the others only jumped over him and came on.

"Hurry up," said Sayen's mother as she guided Erielle up the stairs.

When they were all inside the stairwell, Sayen locked the door. They stepped out onto the windswept roof.

Smoke was rising up all around them into the early morning sky.

To one side, where the helis had stood, was a pile of smoking ruins. A missile had destroyed the helis. They weren't much more than lumps of charred, twisted, reeking metal. "Krat," exclaimed Sayen's mother. They walked slowly over to what was left of their only means of escape.

"What now?" Carl asked.

Sayen's father turned to him with a stricken expression. "I'm all out of answers to that question, son."

Sayen swallowed. "Daddy, Mama, it's okay. We did what had to. We've done all we could." She put Makey down so that she could embrace them both. Then she turned and hugged Erielle, holding onto the stubborn, pigheaded, dogmatic woman as if she were life itself.

Jas and Carl looked at each other and smiled briefly. They turned, raised their weapons, and aimed them at the door on the other side of the roof, waiting for the Shadows to emerge.

A blast of hot air swept down from above, and over the roar of the burning house came the whine of a shuttle engine.

"Krat," shouted Jas. "They're coming at us from above too." She turned and aimed at the floor of the shuttle that hung over them. A tiny escape hatch opened, and the head and shoulders of a man appeared in the space.

As Jas sighted her gun, Sayen ran at her and knocked her down.

"What the...?" she exclaimed from the floor.

"Phelan," yelled Sayen. "Mama, Daddy, it's Phelan. Back up, everyone, so they can land."

"They can't land on the roof. It'll only burn the place down faster," Carl shouted over the engine's whine.

"Not our roof," Mrs. Lee called in reply. "But we'll have to take shelter from the heat of the engines. I think Phelan was trying to warn us."

"Over here," Mr. Lee said, and he led them to a raised section. Sayen picked up Makey and carried him over. They hid on the side facing away from the descending shuttle. Nevertheless, the air turned very hot as the aircraft fired its landing jets.

When the shuttle's noise was quiet, they ventured out. A couple of Shadows must have tried to emerge onto the roof as the shuttle was landing. Their lobster-red, blistered remains were contorted into tortured shapes. They made their way across the roof. The shuttle door opened, and Sayen's brother, Phelan, came out.

"Hurry," he called, gesturing at them. "This place is going up in flames. We don't have long before it collapses."

Sayen ran to her brother, who took Makey from her before disappearing inside the shuttle. Jas and Carl helped Erielle as she shuffled along on her crutches. Mr. and Mrs. Lee brought up the rear. Crashes and explosions came from the disintegrating mansion beneath them. Suddenly, a portion of the roof collapsed, a jet of flame leapt up, and the shuttle began to slide toward the hole.

"Come on," yelled Phelan, gripping the door edge for support in the angled, moving shuttle. He waved frantically at them with his other hand and moved aside as Jas and Carl arrived at the door and helped Erielle through. Sayen stepped aboard, then turned to check on her parents.

Her mother was right behind her, but with horror she saw that Shadows were pouring onto the roof, and that her father had stopped to fire at them, trying to hold them off so the others could get away. Her mother noticed Sayen's expression and turned back to see her husband's plight.

"Craven," she screamed.

"Go," he shouted over his shoulder.

The shuttle was sliding inexorably toward the hole. "Inside, Sayen, Mama," yelled Phelan. "Now."

He pushed Sayen in and tried to pull his mother aboard the shuttle, but the woman shook him off. "I've been with that man for forty years. I'm not abandoning him now." She gave her son a mighty push, sending him through the shuttle doors. The aircraft was at a precarious angle, and everyone was slipping down the floor.

Sayen had fallen down in the entranceway and was staring at her brother in shock. Phelan slammed the doors shut. The engines fired, and they were airborne.

16

Jas went to comfort Sayen, but she was inconsolable. She sat on the floor, sobbing and rocking in almost animal-like despair. Her brother was white-faced and trembling. He was shaking his head, as if trying to rid himself of the memory of the last few minutes. After a while, he sat with his sister, and they held each other.

No one spoke. Everyone but Makey was in the entranceway of the shuttle. Away from the heated air and the roar of the burning mansion, the quiet, cool interior of the spacecraft seemed almost surreal. Its flight was easy and smooth.

Finally, Phelan composed himself a little. He held his sister's shoulders and looked into her face. "When I got the packet from Mama saying you'd gone missing," he said, "I came as fast as I could, but I was on the other side of the galaxy."

Sayen nodded and wiped her eyes.

"I'm glad you're safe," said Phelan.

Jas, Carl, and Erielle went into the passenger cabin to give them some time together. There were only eight passenger seats in the small craft. Jas sat down and wondered what it was that Sayen's brother did that took him across the galaxy. She hadn't noticed a company logo on the side of the shuttle.

Makey had been deposited in a seat. He was awake but disoriented. Jas inspected the already deep purple, large bruise on his forehead. She hoped there were medical facilities wherever it was that the shuttle was taking them.

"Are you okay?" Carl asked her. When she nodded, he said, "I'm gonna talk to the pilot." He left her with Erielle and the kid.

The underworlder was looking better after her short stint of care at Sayen's home. She was clearly troubled, however. She glanced repeatedly at the doorway to the shuttle's entrance, obviously concerned about Sayen.

Jas sat back in her seat and stared unseeing in front of her. Mr. and Mrs. Lee didn't stand a chance, of course. Even if they survived the searing heat of the shuttle's engines and they defeated the attacking aliens, there was no way they would make it out of the burning building alive.

They were such wonderful people. So smart and wise, and they loved their family so deeply. The world would feel their loss. *She* felt their loss, and she'd hardly known them. She wanted to weep for them, but as usual, the tears wouldn't come.

Yet the ache in her heart had to be nothing compared to how Sayen and her brother must be feeling. It was at times like these the fact that Jas had no family that she knew of brought her some small comfort. She missed out on the warmth, closeness, and love that most families seemed to experience, but she also missed out on losing them.

Carl reappeared from the pilot's cabin. He sat next to Jas and fastened his seat belt.

"How's the kid?" he asked.

"He needs medical care."

Carl nodded. "He should get it soon. I talked to the pilot. It turns out Sayen's brother owns a deep space mining company. His starship's in orbit, and we're going to it now."

"They've been in deep space for the last few months?" Jas asked.

"Looks like it."

"So it's unlikely they have any Shadows aboard?"

"I think so. The pilot had no idea what I was talking about. Never heard of Shadows. Never seen a trap."

For the first time in what seemed like forever, Jas relaxed. For the immediate future, she wouldn't have to worry about encountering one of the hostile aliens. She wouldn't have to wonder if the person she was speaking to really was who they appeared to be.

What was more, they'd done what they set out to do: they'd alerted the Transgalactic Council. Yet somehow, she couldn't take any pleasure in the achievement. So many lives had been lost. The Shadows were even abducting children and replacing them with weird, animal-loving dopplegangers.

Carl reached out and took her hand. He folded his fingers over hers.

"After we get to Phelan's ship?" she asked him. "What then? What do we do next?"

"I don't know. I have to go and get Flux, for one thing. The little fella probably thinks I'm dead. After that, I'm not sure. I don't want to abandon the farm, especially if the Shadows have plans for it, but Earth isn't safe anymore."

"No, it isn't. When the Transgalactic Council receives the packet, what do you think they'll do?"

"They'll have to react. If they don't stop the Shadows from taking over Earth, the rest of the galaxy will be next."

They lapsed into silence. The shuttle flew on, taking them farther from their alien-infested world and closer to their temporary safe haven.

Carl's fingers loosened their grasp on hers. Jas looked at him and found that he'd fallen asleep. She was glad to see that peace had settled on his face.

But then, despite their miraculous escape, and despite the fact that they were on their way to the first safe place they'd known since the *Galathea* had landed on K. 67092d, a chill settled over her heart. There was only one way the Transgalactic Council could react. They would have to go on the offensive to decisively rid the galaxy of the Shadows' menace.

War was coming, and somehow Jas knew that she, Carl, and their companions would find themselves caught up in it.

JAS'S STORY CONTINUES IN

MARS BORN

SHADOWS OF THE VOID BOOK 8

&

THE GALACTIC CHRONICLES
SHADOWS OF THE VOID BOOKS 8 – 10

Sign up to my reader group for a free copy of *Starbound*, the
Shadows of the Void prequel that tells the story of what
happened to Jas Harrington in Antarctica, and for exclusive
notice of new releases, advanced reader opportunities and
other interesting stuff:

https://jjgreenauthor.com/free-books/